Copyright © 2015 by Jessica Sorensen

For information: jessicasorensen.com

Cover Photo and Design by Maeidesign

Entranced (Guardian Academy, Book One)

ISBN: 978-1519516244

D0547754

Chapter 1

I'm the only human in the club. Well, except for Jayse Hale, my cousin and best friend on the entire planet. Although, human might be a stretch, considering we have Keeper's blood pumping through our veins. At least, I'm pretty sure I do.

Technically, I haven't gotten my Keeper's mark yet, but Jayse has. The fiery ring of gold showed up on his shoulder almost a year ago when he turned sixteen. His parents, my Aunt Aislin and Uncle Laylen, were ecstatic he inherited inhuman strength. It comes in useful for endeavors like tonight, when almost every creature near us is inhumanly strong and can easily kill an average person.

My parents, Alex and Gemma Avery, keep telling me it's only a matter of time before my mark shows up. My mom, dad, and over half of my extended family bear the mark of a Keeper—warriors who protect the human race from all those scary things that go bump in the night. Things most people don't believe exist. Believe me; they do exist. But, thanks to us lovely Keepers who kick ass and risk our lives daily, most people get to live their lives without ever crossing paths with vampires, werewolves, fey, and all kinds of otherworldly creatures.

Me, I get to stand in a room crammed with them.

The Black Dungeon is one of the many clubs in the city exclusively for anyone and everything who like to dip their feet, fangs, third eyes, or etc. into the dark side. The dress code to get in requires dark clothing, which is why I'm rocking a tight black tank, black jeans, and a pair of lace-up, thigh-high boots that make my already long legs look even longer. On top of that, you have to possess the Mark of Immortality. Jayse and I aren't immortal, but thanks to Blaire, Jayse's younger sister who has badass Wicca skills, we have temporary marks on our forearms, an illusion created by a magic spell. My unearthly violet eyes also give me an edge, the strangely unique color inherited from my mom and my grandpa Lucas.

"What are we looking for exactly?" Jayse asks me as we dance to the bass-driven song.

Lights shimmer above us, and a faint mist floats around my feet as I skim the sea of faces near me. Most of them appear to be human, but if I look closely enough, I can spot glowing eyes, scaly skin, and claws for hands. "We're looking for someone. I already told you that."

He leans in, coughing as the mist swirls up to our faces. "You keep saying someone, but clearly that someone is a something, so fess up." He moves back, his bright blue eyes sparkling with amusement. Like me, he's dressed from head to toe in black with studs on his belt and bands on his wrists, making him appear like an edgy, bad boy from the neck down, but his bright blue eyes and messy blond hair give him a pretty-boy look. "Alana Avery, what kind of trouble are you getting us into this time?"

"If I tell you, then you have to promise not to give me a big lecture on making bad choices." Even though I'm five-nine, I have to tip my chin to look up at him—he's that tall. "I've heard it way too many times."

His lips quirk. "Well, if you didn't make so many bad choices, I wouldn't have to lecture you all the time."

"That or you could just accept that your awesome best friend sometimes does crazy stuff, but it almost always plays out in our favor."

"One day, it's going to catch up with us."

"Maybe you should stop coming with me if you're so worried."

"Imagine how much trouble you'd get into if I did," he says with an arch of his brows.

"I can take care of myself." I squint against the lights vibrantly flashing with the beat of the song. "Everyone thinks that just because I don't have my mark, I can't protect myself. I know what I'm doing. I'm not weak." Everyone forgets that I've been in this life since I was born.

His expression softens. "No one said you are. We know you're tough. We just care about you. Until you get the mark, so much bad stuff can still happen to you."

I tuck a strand of my long, brown hair behind my ear. "I know. I'm sorry for complaining. I just get so frustrated sometimes."

He shifts closer and whispers, "Is that why we're here? So you can try to prove you can take care of yourself?"

"It's freakin' scary how well you know me," I say with a defeated sigh.

"I'd be the biggest asshole if I didn't. I mean, we've been best friends since we could walk. That's a freakin' long-ass time."

I nod in agreement.

Our parents are best friends, and his mom is my dad's sister, so we were kind of predestined to be best friends. It's probably a good thing, too. While I like to do crazy, dangerous things, Jayse is more levelheaded and keeps an eye on me. He always seems to know when I'm up to something, like tonight.

The main reason I came to the Black Dungeon is because I heard Anastasiya is supposed to be here. She has major status in the vampire world and is the cause behind a ton of human deaths. The Keepers have wanted to get their hands on her for a while, but she typically stays off the radar and has a ton of bodyguards surrounding her when she does make her presence known.

"So, who are you trying to find?" Jayse asks, inching closer as sweaty bodies start to crowd us.

I pull a guilty face, nudging someone when they bump into me. "Anastasiya."

His eyes widen. "Please tell me you're joking. That you didn't come here tonight to try and execute ..." He casts a panicked glance around at the mob then leans in toward me. "We'll never be able to kill her. She's too powerful."

"Not if we can get her alone," I hiss under my breath. "She's only powerful because she has her precious bodyguards. Take them away, and she's just a regular, old vampire."

"No vampire is just a regular, old vampire." Frustration fills his voice. "And even if we could take her, her guards never leave her alone."

"That's not completely true. I know for a fact that, sometime around midnight, she'll be on the roof alone all by her little old self."

"How do you know that?"

"Um ..." I chew on my lip guiltily. "I may have been tipped off by someone who can see into the future."

"You talked to *Elliot*?" His jaw ticks. "You know he's not a reliable Foreseer. He probably lied to you to set you up."

"He wouldn't do that to me, Jayse ... I know everyone doesn't like Elliot, but he's not as bad as everyone thinks. He just messed up that one time and no one will forgive him."

"Messed up that *one time*. He tried to mess around with visions when he knew he wasn't supposed to and almost set off an apocalypse. And the only reason that didn't happen is because he was caught before he actually went through with it."

"That was a long time ago, back when he was still learning how to control his psychic abilities. Even you messed up a lot when you were training," I say. "Jayse, I'm really sorry, but I need to do this. You don't understand the pressure I'm under from my mom and dad. They keep saying shit like, 'When is Alana's mark going to show up?' And, 'If she doesn't get one, we're going to have to send her somewhere safe.' It's starting to worry me."

He gapes at me. "They're talking about sending you

away?"

I nod. "For my senior year. They think I should go to some boarding school across the country."

"But you can't move." His lips pull to a sad smile. "My life would be way too dull without you."

"So you'll help me with this, then? Let me prove I'm stronger than everyone thinks?" I clasp my hands in front of me. "Please say yes, Jayse."

He offers me an apologetic look. "I don't want you to move away, but I can't let you go through with this. It's too risky. I'm sorry, but I'm texting for back up." When I start to open my mouth, he talks over me. "I'm not arguing. I'm not going to let you risk your life."

"We take risks like all the time. This isn't any different."

"Taking on"—he lowers his voice as he slips his hand into his pocket, retrieving his phone—"Anastasiya ... You'll get yourself killed." He punches a few buttons on his phone. "We'll find another way to keep you from moving, okay?"

So much for proving I'm a badass. Texting for backup means a ton of Keepers are going to show up soon and take over the situation.

"They'll still let you help," he tries to reassure me.

I force a smile. "Yeah, maybe."

He's wrong, though. Since my parents hold high status in the Keepers' circle, everyone knows me, knows that I don't have my mark yet, and that I'm not supposed to be working any jobs.

He stuffs the phone into his back pocket of his pants. "They're on their way. I have to stick around until they get here ... Do you want to go home?"

I shake my head as we start to dance again. "No, but are my parents included in the 'they'?"

He stares at something over my shoulder. "I don't think so."

"I hope not or my ass is going to get grounded. Then I won't get to see you before I move away." I swallow the lump wedged in my throat.

I know I'm acting like a baby, but the idea of moving away from my family, from Jayse, from the life I've always known is killing me. I thought tonight would at least give me a chance at being able to stay. Now that chance is rapidly slipping away from me.

Tonight wasn't supposed to go down like this. Usually, Jayse goes along with my plans, even if they're dangerous. Lately, though, he's acting more responsibly. I blame it on the mark. It changed him, made him like every other Keeper.

The day he got his mark, I felt like I lost my best friend. Sure, I still love Jayse to death and I'd do anything for him, but I can feel a wall between us, dividing how we view situations.

I miss my old best friend who said to hell with everything and held my hand as we jumped blindly into danger.

If only the stupid mark would just appear! Then shit could go back to normal.

As if reading my mind, the back of my neck begins to burn, like a tattoo needle buzzing away, inking my flesh. This has to be it—my mark appearing! Of course, I need to go check before I declare it since I've had more than a handful of false alarms.

"I have to go to the bathroom!" I shout to Jayse over the music.

He glances at the clock then shoots me a dubious look. "It's almost midnight. Are you sure you're not just trying to sneak off to the roof?"

I press my hand to my chest, mocking offense. "You think I'd lie to my best friend?"

He gives me a blank stare. "Do I really need to answer that?"

"Oh, fine, but I only lie to you when I'm trying to protect you." I back away from him with my elbows out, making a path through the throng. "I'm not lying, though. I really do need to pee." I smile sweetly at a guy with glittery gold hair who shoots me a disgusted look. "What? Don't pretend like you don't do it, too."

He actually might not, depending on what he is. With the crazy hair and shimmering skin, my bet is a Pixie.

The Pixie in question rolls his eyes then turns back to the woman with snow-white hair that he's dancing with.

I smile proudly at Jayse. "See? I know how to ease over situations."

He fights back a grin. "Go to the bathroom and meet me at the bar when you're done."

I spin around and squeeze through the sweaty bodies, making my way to the back of the club. As I pass by a freakishly tall, very well built guy with jet-black hair, he grabs my waist and tries to grind himself all up in my business. The skin-to-skin contact from his palm creeping up the front of my shirt makes me gag.

I push him away, jabbing my shoulder into his chest. "Dude, I'm not into vampires. Sorry."

He flashes me his fangs. "I bet I can change your mind," he purrs, leaning in like he's going to bite me.

I splay my fingers across his face and shove him back.

Entranced

"No way. Never gonna happen."

He hisses at me, and my heart slams against my chest. But on the outside, I remain cool, despite the fact that the vampire could go all off-with-her-head on me if needed.

Squaring my shoulders, I brush by him, nudging him out of the way when he gets all up in my personal space again. He growls, but thankfully doesn't chase after me.

I push my way off the dance floor, the mist fading as I make it to the dimly lit table area. I don't make eye contact with the vampire feasting off the human's neck in the far corner booth, but my fingers itch to draw out my knife from my ankle sheath, and stake him in the heart. If I knew for sure I had my mark, I just might give it a go. Instead, I keep my hands fisted to my sides, duck down a dimly lit hallway, and slip into the bathroom.

As the door swings shut behind me, the lights flicker. I worry the power might go off and smother me in darkness before I get to see if I have the mark.

The lights end up staying on, and I stride toward a row of mirrors above the sink bowls, checking under each stall on my way to make sure I'm alone. The last thing I need is for anything to see the mark on my neck.

Once I'm positive no one else is in here, I turn my back to the mirror, sweep my hair to the side, and then instantly frown.

"Dammit." The only thing marking my flesh is a blotchy, red spot, which probably came from early when a Faerie bumped me in the back of the neck with his wing.

I let my hair fall over my shoulder and grip the edge of the sink bowl. I know it won't be the end of the world if it turns out I'm not a Keeper, but it'll separate me from my friends and family. It already kind of has. I've become a burden, a constant concern to everyone I love, and deep down, I don't blame my parents for wanting to send me away from this lifestyle. They want to protect me; I get that. It just sucks balls big time.

Suddenly, the doors behind me swing open and a short, curvy woman with flowing red hair and bloodstained lips stumbles in. The fangs descending from her mouth and dry blood on her chin reveal she's a vampire.

She's riding a blood high, but when she spots me, the glazed look in her eyes diminishes. She skims me over, her nostrils flaring as she inhales deeply. I know she's trying to get a vibe on what I am. She won't get one, thanks to the magic bound inside my temporary Mark of Immortality.

I stare her down, waiting for her to say something, call me out, try to eat me, whatever she plans on doing. My hands are at my sides, fingers ready to snatch the knife from my ankle sheath, but she ends up giving up and stomps into a stall, slamming the door behind her.

A slow exhale eases from my lips as I unstiffen.

I check the time on my phone. Almost midnight.

"Shit." I hurry out of the bathroom a little too fast and end up crashing into someone.

"Watch it," a guy snaps as I trip backward from the impact and bash my elbow against the wall.

Classy spazz move, Alana. You're going to give away that you're a clumsy human.

The scents of cologne, soap, and something woodsy flood my nostrils as I regain my footing. I know that scent. This dude is a werewolf.

Despite the angry scowl he's sporting, I admit the guy is sort of cute. Okay, maybe more like freakin' hot. He's maybe a couple of years older than me, tall, with light brown hair styled in a messy fauxhawk. Intricate tattoos wind around his lean arms and up his neck, and he has the craziest, most intense silver eyes I've ever seen. Although, the shade does seem oddly out of place, considering silver is a werewolf's kryptonite and most have brownish gold or bright yellow eyes.

Werewolf dude glares at me. "Do the world a favor and learn how to walk."

17

Okay. He *so* just lost a few sexy points for that remark.

"Sorry." My voice drips with sugary sweetness. "I've tried a ton of times to get my how-to-walk learner's permit, but the instructor always fails me because I keep crashing into brooding guys who never seem to know how to watch where *they're* walking. It's a curse. Seriously."

He stares at me, unimpressed, with his arms folded. "I'm not brooding; I'm just in a hurry."

I gesture for him to get a move on. "Well, then you should probably get going instead of wasting time insulting my walking incompetence." When he continues to stare me down, I put my hands on my hips and arch my brows at him. "What? Never had anyone call you out before?"

"No, but if they did, I'd make them shut hell up." His gaze drops to the markings on my arm, and then his head cocks to the side. "I'm just trying to decide if I want to shut you the hell up."

I keep a calm expression, but I'm a little frazzled on the inside. He glanced at the Mark of Immortality. Can he tell it's fake?

I shove the thought from my head. No, if he knew I was human, he probably would've killed me already. Not all werewolves are completely bad, especially in human form, but werewolves who hang out at places like the Black

18

Dungeon are usually looking for trouble.

"What? Cat got your tongue?" he questions with a smirk. "Or should I say wolf?"

I roll my eyes. "That was super cheesy. Seriously, dude, does that ever work on anyone?"

His smirk broadens. "It got you flustered, didn't it?"

I roll my eyes again. "Well, it's been a real pleasure running into you, but I've got other broody guys to run into."

I start to walk away, waggling my fingers at him, but his fingers wrap around my arm. Moments later, his breath dusts the back of my neck.

"Don't do it," he whispers in a low tone that carries a warning. "You'll end up getting killed."

"I'm not doing anything except trying to get away from you." I try to slip my arm from his hold, but he tightens his grip. A shallow breath escapes my lips. "Let. Me. Go."

"Stay away from Anastasiya, Alana"—his voice is one step away from a growl—"because, if you get in my way, I'll have no choice but to kill you, which would be a real waste considering you're the first person I ever let walk away from me unscratched after calling me a cocky asshole." With a brush of his fingers across the back of my neck, he mutters, "Interesting," then moves away from me.

I spin around with my hand cupped over the back of my neck.

"Don't look so worried." He backs down the hallway in the opposite direction of the dance floor, stuffing his hands into the pocket of his black cargo pants. "I promise you and I'll run into each other again very soon. I just hope by then you've learned how to walk better." With that, he turns around and pushes out the Do Not Enter door at the end of the hallway.

I stare at the door with my jaw hanging to my knees and a thousand questions racing through my mind. What the hell just happened? How the hell does he know what I'm plotting tonight? How does he know who I am? Better yet, how the hell does he know we're going to meet again?

Chapter 2

By the time I make it to the bar, a handful of Keepers have arrived. They aren't near each other to keep under the radar—some are on the dance floor, others near the serving table.

Jayse is chatting with the bartender when I approach him. He seems cheerier than when I last saw him, laughing at something the woman behind the counter says. She looks a few years older than him with flowing red hair. From the way he keeps throwing her charming smiles, I can tell he's flirting with her.

Usually, I'd tease the crap out of him, but I'm too worried about Wolf Guy.

When Jayse catches sight of me, his expression sinks. "What happened?" He examines my face. "You look pale? Are you getting a fever?" He places his palm to my forehead.

I dip my head away from his hand. "Stop being a weirdo," I hiss under my breath as I worriedly peer around the

21

club. "We're being watched." I slump onto a barstool.

"By who?" He sits back down, still watching me as if I'm made of cracking glass.

I slant forward in the chair. "I ran into a werewolf in the hallway. Somehow, he knows why I came here tonight."

He jerks back, his eyes flooding with panic. "I need to warn everyone."

"Jayse, I don't think—"

He's already hurrying off toward a group of Keepers on the dance floor.

Sighing, I get up to warn the Keepers lounging around in the serving area.

Tonight turned into a disaster. I left my house with such high hopes that I could pull off some badassary and prove I'm a warrior, even without the mark, but all I managed to do was get everyone into a sketchy situation.

I warn the Keepers to bail out, and they seem super irritated with me.

"Stupid girl needs to stay out of our business," one of them says, glaring at me. "You're not a Keeper just because your parents are. Are you trying to get people killed?"

When the other two nod in agreement, my muscles wind into knots. I'm fuming mad. But under the anger, I feel embarrassed because I know everything they're saying is true.

Unable to stand and endure the scrutiny any longer, I turn around and push my way to the exit of the club

After I make it outside, I wait for Jayse in the alleyway in front of the entrance. The full moon shimmers brightly in the dark sky and the air is still except for the faint sounds of cars driving up and down the nearby road. While I'm used to being alone in strange, creepy places, the werewolf's words haunt my mind.

Werewolves aren't known for having mind reading skills. That trait usually applies to witches and foreseers. So how did he know what I was up to? He could've overheard me when I was talking to Jayse, but I don't recall seeing him anywhere near the dance floor.

A scream abruptly cuts through the air, tearing through my thoughts. My gaze darts upward just in time to see a figure tumbling down from the roof.

I skitter across the alley to the other side, barely making it out of the way before the body hits the ground right where I was standing only seconds ago.

"Holy shit," I breathe as I stare at the unmoving body.

Drawing my knife from my boots, I dare an inch or two closer, trying to see who or what it is.

They're facedown, blood pooling around their head, and the long, brown hair splayed across the ground has me guessing it's a woman.

Sucking in a breath, I crouch down to get a better look. I've seen dead bodies before, but never one this mangled: skin torn up, gaping holes in her stomach, like someone took a giant bite out of her. I feel a sick to my stomach. Still, I find myself wanting to examine her more closely, try to figure out what happened. The fall definitely isn't what killed her, and the injuries had to have been done to her beforehand.

I carefully roll her over onto her back then gasp. *Anastasiya*. "Holy shit!"

What the hell? Did one of the Keepers go through with the plan? No, if they'd staked her, she'd have turned to ash. The cause of death … It has to be the claw and bite marks, which can only mean one thing.

A howl from above rings through the air, confirming my suspicion. I step away from the dead vampire and look up at the roof where glowing, silver eyes stare through the darkness at me.

"I know you," I say. "You're the guy from inside, aren't you?"

The wolf lets out another howl, throwing his head up at

the sky, before backing away from the ledge of the roof and vanishing from sight.

"Okay, I think everyone cleared out," Jayse announces as he exits the club. "Let's get out ..." He trails off, drifting to a stop. "What the hell ...?" He shakes his head, gaping from Anastasiya to me. "Alana, what did you do?"

I pause for a microsecond, debating whether to take the credit for this. I can't lie to Jayse without feeling guilty, though, so I decide not to try.

"I didn't do anything," I tell him, stealing a glance at the roof again.

He appears unconvinced. "Then how the hell did Anastasiya end up dead at your feet?"

"If I staked her then there wouldn't be a body."

"That's not the only way to kill a vamp, and you know it. You could've poisoned her, beheaded her." His gaze drops to the body. "Although, her head is intact."

I sigh then give him a brief rundown of what just happened.

"So, you think it was the same wolf you ran into in the club?" Jayse asks after I'm done explaining.

I shrug, retuning my knife to my ankle sheath. "He had the same silver eyes, but he was totally rocking his hairy beast, fangs, four legs wolf suit, so I couldn't tell for sure."

Jayse rubs his jawline, contemplatively glancing from the roof to the woman. "I think we need to call the Guardians and have them come take a look."

I instinctively pull a face. Guardians are investigators for murders committed in the paranormal world. They're very analytical and always ask way too many questions. In my opinion, it's one of the worst titles a person can get, and many Keepers would agree with me. Spending time examining dead bodies without actually fighting anything—no one is ever too thrilled to get that position. No one sane, anyway.

"You don't know for sure if she was murdered," I say to Jayse. "And she could've attacked the wolf first or he was just defending himself."

He gives me the look he always gives me whenever I'm being difficult and he's trying to tolerate me. "I get that no one likes the Guardians, but we need to follow protocol."

"But you know how they are. They'll end up questioning me until they think they've pried every single detail out of me, and I don't have time for that," I explain with a frown. "I'm supposed to go archery shooting with my grandpa in the morning. We're having a competition, too. Winner gets a hundred bucks. I want that hundred bucks, but I'll never be able to win if I'm so tired that I can't keep my eyes open."

"Alana, you know the rules. If it looks like a murder, then we have to call it in." He retrieves his phone from his pocket to make the call.

"Fine, but just for the record, I miss the old rule-breaker Jayse," I tell him as he paces the alley with the phone pressed to his ear.

"Yeah, but you still love me," he replies with a grin.

I roll my eyes, not arguing, because he's right. I'll always love Jayse, and he'll always be my best friend, even if I'm going to lose a hundred bucks because of him.

Chapter 3

An arrow springs forward from my bow and smacks the target with a *thwack,* slamming too far away from the bullseye. I stifle a yawn as I lower the bow to my side, frustrated over how exhausted I am.

I was right about the Guardians. By the time I finished answering their questions, it was nearing sunrise. I probably got a total of two hours of sleep before I had to wake up to go shooting with my grandpa Lucas.

"You seem tired," Grandpa Lucas remarks with an I'm-so-gonna-win-this-competition smile. Like me, he's competitive, so he isn't going easy on me just because I'm his granddaughter. "Stay out too late?"

"Like you don't already know the answer," I say in a teasing tone. My archery skills may suck today, but that doesn't mean I've lost the ability to joke around with my grandpa, who's one of my favorite people in the world. "I know my mom and dad told you all about my little stunt last night. You may think you were talking quietly, but my teenage hearing is way better than your old people hearing."

He shoots me a joking scowl. "Hey, I'm not that old." He raises the bow with an arrow loaded, shoots it straight into the center of the target, and then grins at me because he just won the competition. "And I can still kick your teenage butt at archery."

I set my bow down, leaning it against my leg while I tug off my mesh glove. "You only won because I'm tired."

"Whatever you need to tell yourself to make you feel better about losing," he says as he removes his gloves.

I give him my best sad, puppy dog eyes. "Are you really going to make me give you a hundred bucks? Because it's pretty much all the money I have."

He raises his brows at me. "Would you make me pay you if I lost?"

I shake my head. "No way. I'm too nice."

"You sure about that?"

"No."

"Then don't you think it's fair that you pay?"

"I guess so." I collect my bow and gloves from off the ground and head back across the field toward the three-story, stone castle that belongs to the Keepers. While I don't call the place home, I probably spend as much time here as I do at my house.

My grandpa Lucas quietly strolls along beside me as I hike through the tall grass, past the glistening lake, and up the steep hillside. When we almost reach the heavy, wooden door of the castle, he stops me before I walk in.

"How about this," he says, "we meet up next weekend and do double or nothing? Just keep in mind that that's two hundred bucks you'll owe me if you lose."

My mood perks up. "Really?"

He nods. "But just make sure you get enough sleep. No staying out and trying to pull crazy stunts."

I nod then throw my arms around him. "Thank you, Grandpa. You're the best."

"Remember that when I'm kicking your butt next weekend," he teases, patting me on the back.

I chuckle as I step back. "In your dreams, old man."

We continue to trash talk each other as we wander inside the castle and down the hallway toward the library where my mom and dad are more than likely working on some sort of Keeper mission. Strangely, though, they aren't there.

We search the entire house, but not a single Keeper is around.

"That's weird," I say as we start back downstairs. "Did

they say they were going somewhere?"

He shakes his head, puzzlement etched deep in his face. "They were actually supposed to talk to me about something when we got back. Maybe they got called out on a job, though."

I glance at the clock on the wall. "But it's only noon." Usually, Keeper missions go down when the sun sets because, for some reason, most creatures seem to be nocturnal.

"I know." His confusion deepens as he descends the stairway.

I trail after him, scratching at the back of my neck. The damn thing has been so itchy today. I'm starting to get worried something stung me last night, and that's why I felt the burning sensation at the club.

"Grandpa, is there a creature that can sting you and make your skin itchy?" I ask as we reach the bottom of the stairs.

"There's a ton of creatures that sting, but most are fatal." He pauses, giving me a worried look. "Why? Did something sting you?"

I press my palm to the back of my neck. "I'm not sure. I felt this burn on the back of my neck last night, and I thought it was ... well, my mark appearing. But when I checked it out, my skin was just blotchy, and now it's really itchy. A faerie wing hit me there, but I don't think they sting, do they?"

He shakes his head, his brows knitting. "Let me see it."

I turn around and move my ponytail out of the way.

He's quiet for a moment before he mutters, "Oh, no."

"What's wrong?"

"Well ... You did get your mark."

"I did?" I fist pump the air then hurry for the mirror.

"Gemma, wait!" my grandpa calls out.

"I just want to see it." I stop in front of a small, oval mirror on the wall at the end of the hallway. I sweep my hair out of the way with a smile on my face. But the smile fades when I see the mark tattooed on the back of my neck.

Instead of the Keepers' ring of fiery gold flames, dark ink forms a compass with arrows pointing out of the edge, and strange, winding symbols fill the inside.

"This can't be right ... What the hell is this?" I already know the answer, though. I just don't want to admit it.

He offers me a remorseful look. "I'm so sorry, Alana, but I think you just became a Guardian."

Chapter 4

I shake my head at least a thousand times. "No, I can't be. I'm supposed to be a Keeper. It's in my blood. Everyone I know is a Keeper. There's no Guardian blood on the Lucas's side or the Avery's. This has to be a mistake."

"You know that's not how things work." He offers me a sympathetic look. "Sometimes blood has nothing to do with it. Sometimes, you're just chosen at random."

"That rarely happens." So why did it happen to me? What's so wrong with me that I didn't get to follow in my family's footsteps?

"But it does happen." He pats my shoulder. "I'm sorry you're disappointed, but it's really not as bad as it seems. Like Keepers, Guardians have a purpose, too."

I know I'm being overdramatic, but I feel like I've let my family down. For as long as I can remember, they've always talked about the day when I'd become a Keeper, my dad especially. He's the one who gave me my first sword and taught me how to use it. And Jayse ... We had such big plans for when we both became Keepers. We were going to fight side by side, protecting the world. Now that plan is ruined.

"I don't even know anything about solving crimes." I suck back the waterworks. *Get your shit together, Alana. Stop having a pity party and find a way out of this.* "I only know how to fight. What the hell am I supposed to do with all my mad fighting skills?"

"You can still use them. You won't be completely out of this war. In fact, you might be farther in than before."

Huh?

"Grandpa, what're you talking about? What war?"

He gets a faraway look on his eyes, zoning off into one of his psychic trances. Normally, he only gets the look when he's gazing into a crystal ball.

Something's wrong.

"Grandpa, are you okay? You seem like you're … I don't know … seeing a vision."

The dazedness diminishes as he forces a tense smile. "Forget what I said, okay? I'm just being a rambling, old man."

I study him closely, noting his uneasiness. "You saw something … in a vision, didn't you? I can tell."

He tries to laugh it off. "You know I can't see visions

without my crystal."

"Yeah, I know, but—"

"No, buts. I said to drop it, so please just drop it." His clipped tone throws me off.

"Okay," I reply quietly.

His irritation fades. "I'm so sorry. I don't know what came over me." He rubs his hand over his head. "I think I didn't get enough sleep last night."

"Maybe you should take a nap," I suggest. "I could use one, too." Maybe then I'll wake up, and this whole thing will be a dream.

He swiftly shakes his head. "We need to find your parents. Tell them the news and celebrate."

I cover the mark on the back of my neck with my hand. "I don't think they're going to want to celebrate this. Keepers are never very happy when someone in their family line gets picked for a Guardian or anything else other than a Keeper."

"I think you'll be surprised how excited your parents will be," he says as he backs down the hallway for the front door. "And they'll always love you, no matter what."

"I know that." I just hope they aren't as disappointed as I am.

Chapter 5

After my mom and dad arrive at the castle from an impromptu vampire lair raid, we drive home. After the four of us sit down at the kitchen table and dish out some ice cream, we break the news to them.

My Grandpa turns out to be right. My parents are happy for me, although my dad is a tad disappointed.

"Are you sure it's the only mark that appeared?" he asks.

"I'm sure." I stir the melted vanilla caramel swirl ice cream I've barely touched. "Trust me, I looked everywhere, like, a thousand times."

My dad frowns as he adds fudge topping to his bowl of vanilla ice cream, but quickly smiles when he notes me watching him.

My mom presses my dad with a stressing look. "Honey, our only daughter just got her mark. Let's not dwell that it wasn't a Keepers' mark and celebrate that she won't have to risk her life all the time. This could turn out to be a very good thing for her."

My dad drags his fingers through his hair with a heavy sigh. "I know that." His eyes suddenly light up as he looks at me. "Hey, all that time we've spent watching crime shows might pay off."

I push the bowl of ice cream away and slouch in the chair, no longer hungry. "Yeah, but I'm not sure I have the stomach for looking at dead bodies. I could barely tolerate the one I saw last night."

"There's more to being a Guardian than just looking at dead bodies, Alana," my grandpa says, absentmindedly stirring his ice cream while staring off into empty space.

"Like what?" I press him, wondering why he has been acting like such a weirdo for the last few hours.

"Like …" When he blinks at me, a layer of mist vanishes from his violet eyes. "Well, you'll find out when you get to the academy."

I straighten in the chair. "*Academy*? What are you talking about?"

My grandpa pulls a whoops face then casts an oh-shit look at my mom. "Gemma, I thought you told her about the Academy."

My mom blasts him with a dirty look. "Alex and I were waiting for the right time … when she wasn't so upset."

"Would someone please tell me what's going on before my head explodes?" I plead.

My mom and dad exchange a look before my mom turns to me. "Sweetie, I know this is going to be hard to hear, but you need to try to remain positive, okay?" She waits for me to nod then takes ahold of my hand, clutching it. "Everyone who gets the Guardian mark is required to attend the Academy for training."

I swallow hard. "Where is this Academy?"

My mom's grip on my hand tightens. "In Virginia."

"But that's clear across the country." My voice cracks.

"It's only for a year," my dad chimes in, trying to sound comforting. "And then you can live wherever you want to."

Tears sting at my eyes. "So, I'm just supposed to, what? Pack all my stuff and move there?"

"Honey, you were already planning on moving, anyway," my mom reminds me. "Really, nothing's changed except you have your mark now."

"I was never planning on moving," I say. "I was going to find a way out of it."

It grows so quiet I can hear the blood roaring in my eardrums.

I shake my head, unsure whether to be angry with them or break down and cry. *I'm not ready to leave my life yet. I love it too much.*

"When do I have to go?"

"Tomorrow," Grandpa Lucas answers. "You'll meet someone at the airport."

I shake my head in denial. "I need more time than that. I'm not ready to leave you guys."

"You need to go now ... It's for your own good." The cloudiness in Grandpa's eyes appears again. "You'll be safer there."

"Safer from what?" I ask, even more suspicious of his odd behavior.

He ignores me. "You should start getting your stuff packed so you'll be ready to go."

No. I'm not ready to leave my family behind. And what about Jayse? I've spent almost every waking hour with him since we were born. In fact, he's practically my only friend. Sure, I have a couple of kinda, sorta friends, but I've never been that great at making friends. I get uncomfortable meeting new people and end up making weird jokes that usually go over peoples' heads.

"Can't you guys find a way around this?" I plead with my mom and dad. "You've got so many connections ...

Can't you just call someone and tell them I can't go? That you need me here? Maybe, if I wait a while, I'll get another mark like Aunt Aislin."

When no one responds, I whisper, "Please don't make me go."

"You know we wouldn't make you go if we didn't have to," my mom says, tearing up. "But we have to follow the rules. It's the same if a daughter or son of a Guardian received the Keepers' mark. We'd make them train with us. If no one ever trained, then there'd be no warriors, no Foreseers, no Guardians, no one to protect the world."

"I won't be protecting the world." I scoot away from the table and stand up. "I'll just be waiting around until something bad happens and then cleaning up the mess."

My mom quickly gets to her feet. "But you get to help track down the killer."

"Yeah, I guess." I don't agree with her, though. I could always run away until this all blows over, but since my grandpa Lucas can pretty much *see* everything, it'd be a pointless effort.

I head out of the kitchen, needing to get some fresh air.

"Where are you going?" My mom rounds the table after me.

I hold up my hand, signaling for her to give me some

room. "To say good-bye to Jayse." Saying it aloud causes tears to flood my eyes, and it takes all of my energy not to let them pour out.

She seems reluctant to let me go. "Text me when you get there, okay?"

I nod then rush out of the room. Once I make it outside, I let the tears flow as I sprint across the field that stretches between my family's house and Jayse's family's.

By the time I reach the front door, I'm sobbing so hard I can barely breathe. I knock on the door before barging inside, something I've done almost every day for years now. The downstairs lights are off, which means his parents are probably out on a mission for the Keepers.

I race upstairs, crossing my fingers Jayse didn't go with them. Before his mark, he hardly ever went, but lately, he's been gone more than he's home.

When I burst into his bedroom and find it empty, a weight crashes down on my chest as I realize how much everything has changed.

And it's only going to change more.

I sink into a recliner near the window, text my mom that I made it to Jayse's, and then hug my legs to my chest.

I want to be strong. Hell, I come from a family of Keepers, Foreseers, and even a witch, so I should be stronger than this. I should be able to face what's ahead of me with my chin held high. But as I sit in Jayse's room, I feel overwhelmingly alone and terrified, like a part of my life is slipping away from me forever.

Chapter 6

I end up falling asleep in the recliner until Jayse eventually wakes me up by giving me a gentle shake.

"Hey," he says when I open my eyes.

I sit up in the chair, stretching my arms above my head as I glance out the window at the sun rising above the mountains. "What time is it?"

He glances at the clock on the nightstand. "A little after six."

I eye over the dirt on his clothes, the traces of blood on his knuckles, and the scratches on his arms, all typical wounds for a Keeper who just went on an outing. "Did you just get back from a mission?"

He nods, exhaustedly sinking onto the edge of his bed. "It was a long, crazy night." He rubs his eyes with the heels of his hands. "We actually had to go into a lair."

My eyes widen. "Since when do you guys raid lairs at night? And why are you guys doing so many raids? My parents went on one earlier yesterday too. Usually, you

43

guys only do, like, four or five a year."

"We've been finding more of them. And going there at night … That was accidental. Something trapped us down there and we couldn't get out."

"Do you know what did it?"

He shakes his head, tracing his finger up and down a scratch on his arm. "We were lucky we got out." He drags his hand through his hair, making the strands go askew. "I love my job and everything, but sometimes it's hard."

"It's good that you get to save people, though. Slaying all those vampires … Think about how many people you saved."

He glances up at me. "You sound upset."

"Something happened last night." I suck in a deep breath. "I got my mark."

He leaps to his feet, bursting with excitement. "You did? That's so fuckin' awesome, Alana. Now we can finally work together." He crosses the room and hugs me.

His enthusiasm makes leaving harder. I've been so worried about losing him, but I didn't even think about how difficult it was going to be on him for me to leave. Same with my parents. I just ran out and fell asleep on my last night with them.

"I didn't get the Keeper's mark, Jayse," I whisper

hoarsely.

He jerks back. "*What?*"

"The mark that appeared, it wasn't the Keepers'."

"Then what was it?"

Sighing, I show him the back of my neck.

He grows quiet for a second. "I know you don't like the Guardians, but I'm sure it's not going to be as bad as you think."

"I have to move, Jayse ... to Virginia to attend their Academy." I wander to the window. "I'm going to be living clear across the country."

"When do you have to leave?" he asks, moving up beside me.

I stare across the foggy field at the two-story home I grew up in. "Today."

"You know I'll visit you all the time, right? If I have to, I'll ask to be put on all jobs on the East Coast."

I smile at him, but it's forced. Jayse knows as well as I do that he hasn't been a Keeper long enough to request being put in certain locations.

"I'm going to miss you." I glance around at the bedroom. Memories are everywhere: the first time Jayse and I stayed up all night watching horror movies, even though we weren't supposed to, when we stole his mom's spellbook and tried to perform a spell, when we promised to be best friends no matter what ... "I won't even know what to do with myself without my partner in crime."

"We'll still see each other all the time," he tries to reassure me. "I'll make sure of it."

I hope he's right—I really do—but I have an unsettling feeling that this might be the last time I see Jayse in a very long time.

Chapter 7

I spend the morning with Jayse and his family, eating breakfast and reminiscing. I wish I could stay longer, but eventually my mom texts me that it's time to come home and pack.

I try not to cry as Jayse walks me across the field to my house, but a few tears escape. I can't help thinking about all the times we've walked across this field to meet up and hang out or to sneak out to some club in the middle of the night. Now we may never get to do it again.

While I want to believe that things won't change, that eventually I'll return home and life will go back to normal, I know it won't. Even before I got my Guardian mark, Jayse and I spent less time in the field.

"Are you sure you can't stay longer?" I ask.

"I'm sorry. I wish I could, but I ..." He presses his lips together, stuffing his hands into his pockets.

"You're doing something for the Keepers today, aren't you?" I make a guess based on how guilty he looks. "You don't need to coddle me. You've been a Keeper for almost a year and have never held stuff back."

"But I feel like such an asshole for even mentioning it."

"I'll be okay... Sure I'm upset, but it doesn't mean I don't want to hear what you're up to."

"It's not just that ... I'm ..." He exhales audibly, staring at the trees surrounding the field. "Now that you have the Guardian mark, I'm not supposed to share certain info with you about my assignments."

I suppress a sigh. *And so it begins.* I knew this was coming. I just didn't imagine it would sting this badly.

"I'm sorry." Jayse glances at me from the corner of his eye. "I wish I could tell you more, but—"

"It's not your fault, so please stop worrying." I give him a stern look. "In fact, promise me you'll stay positive and be the most badass Keeper ever."

He smiles through a chuckle. "Okay, but only if you promise me you'll text me every single day."

We reach my house, and I step onto the bottom porch stair but don't head in, not ready to say good-bye just yet.

"Of course I will," I say. "Just remember, though, when you get tired of me texting you at all sorts of crazy hours, that you were the one who gave me permission to do it."

"Sounds like a deal." He gives me probably one of the saddest smiles I've ever seen then moves in to hug me.

"Kick some ass for me, okay?" I say as he moves back. "But don't work too hard. You look really tired right now."

He smashes his lips together as his gaze drops to his scratched arm. "Yeah, last night was pretty intense …" He looks back at me with a stiff smile on his face. "Be easy on yourself, okay? Don't beat yourself up because you didn't get your Keepers' mark." Hope fills his eyes. "And, hey, maybe the mark will eventually show up, and then you'll get to come home."

"Maybe." But the more it sinks in that I'm now a Guardian, the less likely it feels that I'll ever get to be anything else.

This is it for me. I can feel it in my bones. Whether I like it or not, my future has been chosen for me.

***

A few hours later, I've packed most of my clothes and anything else I could stuff into the two suitcases I'm allowed to bring with me.

"Do you have everything you need?" my mom asks. She's been rocking the mascara-raccoon-eye look ever since I showed up from Jayse's this morning and keeps hugging me every few minutes. "I don't want you to forget anything."

I grasp the handle of my suitcase, taking one last final look at my purple walls covered with posters and photos, my bed, and the field just outside my window. "I think so."

She dabs her eyes with her fingertips. "We should get going. We're supposed to meet your escort at the airport in an hour."

"I wish grandpa could just Foresee me there." I want to look back at my room again as we step out, but I'm afraid I'll start to cry. "I've never flown before."

"You'll be fine," my mom reassures me as we head for the stairway. "Guardians aren't too fond of using Foreseer transportation or any transportation outside of the human world."

My expression plummets. "Human transportation? That sounds complicated."

"It's not that bad." She gathers her long, brown hair into a ponytail and secures it with an elastic as she starts down the stairway. "And it might be good for you to try more complicated stuff without the help of magic."

"That doesn't sound very fun," I say, dragging my suitcases down the stairs.

My grandpa and dad are waiting for us in front of the

door, whispering about something in low voices. When they notice my mom and me, though, they immediately grow quiet.

"Life can't always be fun." She collects the car keys from the pocket of her jeans.

"That's not completely true." My dad smiles at me. "Everything can be fun if you make it."

"Are you quoting one of Grandma's inspirational blocks?" I tease, trying to lighten the mood.

He chuckles, but his green eyes carry worry. "Okay, you caught me, but it's true. If you think you're going to have fun, then you will." He puts a hand on my shoulder, giving me his best you're-going-to-be-okay look. "Stay positive, Alana, and everything will be okay."

I sure hope he's right, but right now, nothing seems like it's going to be okay.

"Where's Grandma?" I ask my grandpa. "Wasn't she supposed to get here last night?"

"I'm sorry, but she got held up with something and isn't going to be home for a couple of days." He reaches into the pocket of his trench coat and digs out a small, silver dagger with a jagged blade. "She wanted me to give you this."

"Dad, I don't think it's a good idea," my mom interrupts. "The Academy Rulebook stressed no weapons outside of one's pre-approved."

"I don't care what the rulebook says. I'm not going to send my granddaughter unarmed to someplace without Keepers nearby," he says. "I've read the rulebook, Gemma. The Guardians don't believe in protection inside the Academy's walls, even when they allow vampires, werewolves, and fey inside."

"Wait, what?" I blink in shock, unsure if I heard him correctly.

"It's their form of protection," my mom explains. "Each human attending there gets paired up with a vampire, wolf, fey, and a few other species so they can be protected. Plus, many of them have great tracking skills."

"I'm strong," I point out. "And I have great tracking skills."

"But not everyone there comes from a family of Keepers." My dad glances at my mom. "I think she should take the dagger."

She sighs in defeat. "Fine, but if she gets caught, you get to explain to the Guardians why we allowed her to take it."

"Fine by me," my dad says as he takes the suitcases from me.

"She won't get caught. This dagger… I had a spell put on it that makes it undetectable from anyone and any machine. Eventually, the magic will wear off, but for now, Alana should be able to carry it around with her." My grandpa sticks out his hand, urging me to take the dagger. "Only use it for emergencies and keep it hidden whenever you can."

I pluck the dagger from his hand, noting the handle and blade have traces of violet swirled through the silver. "I highly doubt I'm going to be running into much while I'm there."

"You should always be prepared for the worst," my grandpa states ominously.

Puzzlement etches my mom's face. "What exactly do you think's going to happen?"

"You take care of yourself, Alana." My grandpa ignores my mom as he hugs me farewell. "And call if you need anything at all."

I nod, hugging him back. "Grandpa, are you sure you're okay? You've been acting weird since yesterday."

He fakes a smile, waving me off. "I'm fine. I'm just little sad. I'm going to miss all of our bets and challenges." I can tell he's hiding something.

"Yeah, me, too."

I don't have too much time to overanalyze his sketchy behavior, though, because my mom announces it's time to go. I say good-bye to my grandpa one last time before we head out to the car.

I fight back the tears as we pull away from the house. My mom cries the entire drive to the airport while my dad remains quiet. Me, I'm stuck in my own worry of what the Academy will be like, whether I'll be able to make friends, or if I'll end up scaring everyone off with my awkward jokes.

I become so lost in my thoughts that I don't realize we've arrived at the airport until my dad opens the door to get out. I unbuckle my seatbelt and meet him around the back of the car to get my bags out.

No one utters a word as we walk from the parking garage to the tunnel that leads to the entrance of the airport. When we're almost to the doors, my mom wraps her arm around my shoulder.

"I thought I was going to have at least another year before you left us."

"Mom, it's going to be okay," I reassure her. "I'll be back before you know it."

Her eyes glisten with tears. "You're handling this much better than I thought you would. After how upset you were last night, I was worried you might try to run away."

"I thought about it," I say as the doors in front of us glide open. "But it wouldn't do any good. You'd either have Grandpa use his Forseeing power to find me or have Aunt Aislin do a tracking spell."

"True, but I'm still glad you decided to handle this maturely," she says as we enter the busy airport.

For her sake, I just hope I can keep it up and don't lose my shit when it's time to take off.

"Where are we supposed to meet them?" I ask as we veer in the opposite direction of the ticket counter. "And don't we need to get my ticket?"

"You're not flying on a main airline," my mom explains as we make our way toward the escalators. "The Academy has their own private jet."

"Is that safe?" I hop onto the moving stairs with her and my dad. "To fly that way, I mean."

My mom casts a quizzical glance at me. "Alana Avery, are you afraid of flying?"

"No." But my thoughts laugh, *liar, liar.* I hadn't realized it until now, but the idea of getting on an airplane makes me feel queasy. "How could I possibly be scared of flying with all the crazy stuff I've done?"

"It's okay to be scared of ordinary stuff," she says.

"Sometimes, ordinary can be scarier when you're not familiar with it."

I want to argue that I'm not scared and put on my brave face, but I get distracted by a guy wearing black cargo pants, a dark T-shirt, and matching combat boots standing at the top of the escalator.

As we near him, his silver eyes lock on me.

Mother-effer.

Wolf guy from the club the other night eyeballs me. It's only when he reaches up to scratch his forehead that I realize why he's here.

"You've got to be kidding me," I grumble to myself as I spot the Guardian mark on his arm.

As if reading my lips, his mouth curls into a grin.

"Asshole," I mutter.

"Alana, watch your language," my mom scolds me as we shuffle off the escalator.

Wolf guy smirks at that. I'm about to tell him to shove his smirk right up his ass when my dad sticks out his hand toward wolf dude.

"Jaxon, it's so nice to see you again. It's too long if you ask me."

"It has, hasn't it?" Wolf Guy—Jaxon—replies, shaking my dad's hand. "And please, call me Jax. Everyone does."

Come again? They know each other?

"How the hell do you know him?" I ask my dad. And since when does my dad shake hands with werewolves?

"Alana, be nice." My dad blasts me a warning look. "Consider yourself lucky that he's going to be your escort to the Academy."

"Gee, lucky me," I say sarcastically, giving a discreet, dirty look in Jax's direction.

He can pretend all he wants, but I know what kind of a guy he really is: the kind who pushes vampires off roofs and threatens to kill me if I get in his way.

He winks at me before facing my dad. "Oh, I'm not just escorting her there, sir." Yep, he actually called my dad sir. Way to kiss ass, wolf guy. "I'm going to be her partner, too."

I grind my teeth. What are the odds of ending up with a guy who not only knew my plan to eliminate Anastasiya and threatened to kill me, but then he killed her himself?

"That's great news." My dad genuinely smiles at me for the first time since I broke the news to him that I'm a Guardian. "I feel so much better about sending you there now that I know you'll be in good hands."

"I thought you weren't worried about me?" I remind my dad.

"Of course I'm worried. You're my only daughter, and while I love you to death, you seem to cause trouble wherever you go. Usually, you have Jayse with you, so I have a little peace of mind, but the idea of you being on your own..." He shakes his head. "Well, I'm just glad you won't be alone."

I peek at Jax who's staring across the airport at the food court then lean in toward my dad, lowering my voice. "For all you know, this guy could be as reckless as me ... You know he's a werewolf, right?"

"I know of the unfortunate incident that happened to him. You don't need to bring it up. Jax's father is a good man. He's helped me out more than a few times."

"You're a good man, and look at how I turned out."

"You turned out fine." But he seems more hesitant now.

"Alana, please behave and be nice to Jax," my mom says, moving between my dad and me. "It'll be easier if you can start this new school with at least one friend. I know how hard it can be for you sometimes."

I want to tell them what happened at the club the other night and see if they remain on the besties-with-Jax page, but I decide to let it drop. It doesn't matter what I say. They'll still make me go to the academy. At least, if I pretend to try to be friends with Jax, they won't worry about me. Besides, if Jax did murder Anastasiya, then technically it's my job to figure out why, not my parents.

My mom takes my silence as an agreement to behave. She turns to Jax, giving him a warm smile. "Jax, it's so nice to meet you. My husband has told me nothing but wonderful things about your family."

"I'm sure he has." Jax returns my mom's smile, but he shifts his weight, seeming uneasy. "I hate to rush you guys, but we do need to get to the plane. Take off is"—he glances at his watch—"in less than an hour."

"Oh, of course." My dad collects my bags and wheels them with him as he heads off with Jax toward a set of gliding doors.

My mom drapes an arm over my shoulder as we follow them. She continuously tells me that everything is going to be okay as we make our way through security and outside to a small plane with a portal stairway pushed up against it.

"Call me every single day and night." She hugs me good-bye, squeezing me so tightly I swear my lungs are going to burst.

"I will," I promise, fighting back the tears.

Eventually, I move away from her arms and say goodbye to my dad. He makes me promise the same thing as my mom before reluctantly letting go. Then I climb the stairs to the plane, waving good-bye to them before ducking inside.

The plane is smaller than I expected with only ten seats, four of which are occupied by three men dressed in dark suits and a woman sporting a collared shirt. They all look at me with annoyance when I walk up the aisle.

"Great, just what we need," the woman says to the man sitting beside her. "A Keeper to corrupt the Academy."

The man shoots me the death glare when he notices me eavesdropping. "Can I help you?"

"Yeah, you can stop insulting my entire family." I refuse to be intimidated by a guy who's probably never fought a day in his life. "If your Academy is corrupt, it has nothing to do with the Keepers."

"You speak highly of a group you're no longer a part of." The woman's eyes narrow on me. "Alana Avery. That is your name, right? Daughter to Alex and Gemma Avery, who from my notes, are fairly high up in the Keepers' circle, and granddaughter to Julian Lucas, a very powerful Foreseer."

I hesitantly nod, wondering where she's going with this. By the way she sneers, I'm guessing it's not going to be pretty.

She leans toward me. "I'm going to let you in on a little secret. All of that may have mattered, but no one at the Academy gives a shit who your parents and grandparents are. In fact, it might be beneficial for you to keep that information to yourself." She shifts back, crossing her legs. "Keepers are nothing but barbaric animals who fight first and think second. Trying to brag only makes you look equally as ridiculous." With that, she starts lightly chatting with the man about where they should have dinner when we land.

Stunned by her rudeness, I wander down the aisle away from them. I've always known most Keepers and Guardians don't get along, but I've never heard a Guardian be so blunt about their hatred for Keepers.

I take an empty seat toward the back, buckle my seatbelt, and stare out the window, watching my parents walk back into the airport. I feel lonely already, and we haven't even taken off yet. How much worse is it going to get?

"It'll get easier." Jaxon plops down in the seat beside me.

I blink my attention from the window. "What will?"

"Leaving your family behind," he says, fastening his seatbelt. "I'm guessing this is probably your first time away from home."

"I'm only seventeen. Most kids my age are still living

with their parents."

The tolerant smile he gives me makes me feel like a child. "Not most Guardians. Most of us leave our families around fifteen or sixteen to attend the Academy."

"How old were you when you went there?"

"Fourteen."

"You were only *fourteen*? That's ... well, really sad."

He simply shrugs. "I got my mark at fourteen. It's not really that uncommon in *our world*."

I frown at the "our world" reference.

"You were a little late getting your mark." He reaches for my neck, grazing his fingers across the mark there and causing me to lose my mind for a second and shiver.

His mouth curls into a smirk, and I jerk back, pointing a finger at him.

"Okay, since we're supposed to be partners or whatever, I need to lay down some rules." I ignore the amusement dancing in his silver eyes as I continue. "The first thing you should know about me is that I'm not really cool with people invading my personal space or putting their hands on me without permission. Got it?"

He nods, his lips twitching to turn upward. "If that's what you want."

"It's what I want." I sound hesitant, though. "And second, I need to know what your deal was the other night." I twist in my seat, bringing my leg up to rest my chin on it. "How did you know about my plan to off Anastasiya?"

His jaw clenches. "How could I not know about it when you and your little friend were blabbering about it so loudly the whole room probably heard?"

"No, we were actually talking pretty quietly, and the music was too loud for your little superpower wolf hearing to work. I know you don't read minds, so fess up. How'd you know?"

His brow cocks. "How do you know I can't read minds? Maybe I have Wicca in me. Did you ever think of that?"

My gaze hastily travels over every ounce of his flesh showing, but his arms and neck are about all I can see.

He reclines back against the armrest and gives me an amused look. "I can take my shirt off if you want to get a better look."

I resist an eye roll. "Or you could just tell the truth."

He drags on the anticipation for a few seconds longer before surrendering. "Look, I'm not a witch, okay? And I didn't overhear you, but I can't tell you how I knew about your stupid plan."

I narrow my eyes at him. "It wasn't stupid. I knew

what I was doing."

"You're not a Keeper or a wolf or a vampire; therefore, it was stupid to think you could kill a vampire as powerful as Anastasiya," he says matter-of-factly.

Anger simmers under my skin. "Don't pretend me being weak is why you stopped me. You only did it so you could kill her yourself, but what I don't get is why a Guardian would kill Anastasiya. I didn't think they killed at all, just found the person who committed the act."

His brows pull together. "What're you talking about? I didn't kill Anastasiya."

"Um, yeah, you did. I saw you on the roof or, well, the wolf you."

"No, you didn't."

"Well, then, it was a wolf who coincidentally had the same silver eyes as you."

His lips thin as he presses them together, no longer looking irritated, but disappointed. "You may have seen a wolf with silver eyes, but it wasn't me."

I pick up one of my bags I tucked under the seat. "Then who was it?"

He shrugs indifferently. "How would I know?"

"You sure look like you know." I unzip the bag and reach inside to grab a bag of licorice. "And whoever it is, I can tell you're disappointed in them."

"Are you sure you're not just a Guardian?" he questions with suspicion. "You seem like you know more than you should."

"Did I ever say I was just a Guardian?" I take a bite of a piece of licorice then smile at him as he eyeballs me with distrust. "Relax, wolf boy." I face forward and prop my feet up on the seat in front of me. "I'm not a Foreseer. My grandfather is one, though, and he sometimes does favors for me, so keep that in mind whenever you feel like lying to me."

He's silent for long enough that I think I've won the argument, but then he grins maliciously. "Before you start worrying so much about me, I'd worry about why Vivianne Monarelle seems so interested with you."

I nibble on the end of the licorice. "Who's Vivianne Monarelle?"

He nods his head toward the front of the plane at the woman who insulted me. She's watching us with interest, and when she sees me looking at her, she glares at me.

"She's in charge of new recruits at the Academy and pretty much runs the training classes. If you get on her bad side, she can make your life a living hell, and with how pissed off she looks right now, I'm guessing you already have. So, good luck with *that*." He gets up and goes to sit up front.

I turn my attention to the window, but I can feel Vivianne staring me during takeoff. Once we're in the air, though, I'm too distracted with freaking the fuck out to care about her.

I've traveled with my grandpa Lucas through a crystal ball before and transported with my aunt so many times I can recite the transporting spell on cue. I even once fell through a portal Jayse's little sister set up as a trap for us when we made her mad and ended up landing in a tree outside the Keepers' castle. None of those forms of transportation are as terrifying as zooming through the sky in a plane controlled by a person.

My fingernails dig into the armrests as the plane jerks, and my muscles are wound so tightly my body aches.

"Never flown before?" Jax plops down in the seat beside me again about thirty minutes into the flight.

I shake my head. "How much longer until we land?"

"About six more hours." He grabs a chip from a small bag he brought with him and pops one into his mouth.

"*Six* more hours of this?" I bite down on my lip as the plane gives another jolt. "Is it going to shake the entire time?"

"It might. It depends on if the storms clears."

A deafening breath escapes me. "This is going to be the longest six hours of my life."

Jax considers something before standing up and leaving me to panic on my own. A minute later, he returns to the seat with a bottle of what I think is water.

"Take a sip of this, and you should be able to sleep through the entire flight."

"What is it?" I stare at it distrustfully. "Vodka or something?"

"A sip of vodka wouldn't knock you out, Alana." He sets the bottle on my lap. "It has Otium in it."

I pick up the bottle and lift it closer to my face to get a better look. Up close, I can see the small flakes of lavender floating around in the clear liquid. "Otium, huh?" I glance at him. "How'd you get this?"

"My grandma's a witch and taught me how to make it," he replies with a half-shrug. "I keep it on hand when I'm on long flights."

"How do I know if it's Otium? What if you're trying to poison me?"

"And why would I want to do that?"

"I don't know." My breath catches in my throat as the plane bumps around. "To keep me quiet about what I saw at the Black Dungeon."

He slants forward, catching my gaze. "I promise I'm not trying to poison you. I'm just trying to help you get through the flight in peace."

He seems honest, but I'm still undecided whether I want to dope myself up with a Wicca herb that will knock me into such a deep sleep nothing will wake me up until it wears off out of my system. But when the plane jerks again and the captain warns everyone to keep their seatbelts fastened, I quickly twist the lid off and take a swig.

"Thanks..." I manage to get out before I black out.

Chapter 8

"Alana, can you hear me?" my grandpa Lucas calls out through the darkness. "Please say you can hear me. I need to talk to you ... God, I need this to work."

I can hear you, *I think to myself.* But where are you?

"Alana!" he calls out, his voice echoing around me. "Please, answer me."

I'm right here! *Grr... I internally growl at myself in frustration. I can't seem to say anything aloud, no matter how hard I try. Where the hell am I? I can't see a damn thing, can't feel my legs, my arms, my mouth ... Maybe that's the problem.*

"I thought this would work," he mutters. "I don't understand."

Taking a deep breath, I slide my feet forward, forcing myself to walk blindly into the darkness. "Grandpa ..." I force my voice out. "I'm ... right ... here."

"Oh, thank God," he says in relief.

I hear the soft pitter-patter of footsteps heading toward

69

me. I don't see him when he reaches me, but I feel his presence nearby.

"I'm glad I was able to meet you here," he says, sounding much closer now.

"Where exactly is here?"

"In one of your dreams."

"You're in my dream*?" My surprise swiftly wears off as I remember my grandpa is a Foreseer. "Is this a new Foreseer thing, being able to enter people's dreams?"*

"We're technically not supposed to," he admits. "But I needed to take the risk."

"Why?"

"Because I need to tell you something important."

"You know, texts work great for that, too, and it's way less creepy."

"I couldn't text you this ... I can't have any sort of trail that'll lead to what I'm about to tell you," he says in that ominous tone again. "If anyone finds out ..." He trails off.

"Grandpa, you're scaring me," I admit. "Before I left, you were acting so strange, and then you show up here ... Please tell me what's going on."

"You're in danger," he whispers, his voice sounding farther away. "Oh no ... I need ... more time ..."

Entranced

"Why am I in danger?" When he doesn't respond, I cry out, *"Grandpa, you're scaring me. Please, just tell me why you think I'm in danger."*

"Because ... they're ..." His voice fades in and out. *"Coming ... after you ... I'm ... sorry."*

"Grandpa!" I shout, my voice echoing around me as I run forward into the darkness. *"Please tell me who they are."*

As the stillness sets in, I begin to panic. Minutes, maybe hours tick by, and I start to fear being trapped here forever when I feel myself slipping back to reality. Right as I'm about to wake up, I feel something cold pressed into my palm, and a single word whispers through my thoughts.

Electi.

Chapter 9

I force my heavy eyelids open and blink away the dizziness swimming in my brain while trying to get my bearings. I'm still on the plane, but the shaking and jolting has stopped. I look out the window at the darkness blanketing the airport and then at the empty seats around me. We've landed, and everyone has vacated the plane, including Jax.

"Gee, thanks for waking me up, guys." I stretch my arms above my head and yawn before collecting my bag from under the seat and getting to my feet.

Thoughts of the trippy dream linger in my mind as I make my way up the aisle and off the plane. I blame it on the Otium. While I've never had it before, witches' potions can have strange side effects, like the time Jayse and I accidentally ate suckers his mom laced with Rabidus Primula to use for a Keeper mission. Jayse and I ended up losing touch with reality and running back and forth across the field for ten hours straight until we were so exhausted we passed out.

Still, as I find my way into the quiet airport, I can't shake the feeling of how real the dream felt, that my grandpa Lucas really did show up to warn me I'm in danger. But in danger from what? An Electi? Because I've never heard of them before, and growing up with Keepers who hunt practically every paranormal creature that exists, it seems like, if they existed, I'd know.

Maybe it's not a creature, though. Perhaps it's something else.

While I wait for my suitcases to show up at the baggage area, I end up sending my grandpa Lucas a text, just to settle my worry. Between how small the airport is and the time nearing ten o'clock, the place is almost empty, so I sit down on the floor and search on the Internet for what electi could be, but I come up with zilch.

"You'll ride with me to the academy," Jax appears by my side out of nowhere.

"Where is everyone else?"

"They had to go downtown for a meeting."

"Okay." While I'm not thrilled to be riding with him, I'm glad I won't be riding in a car with Vivianne.

"And fyi, you talk in your sleep," Jax says. "You say really strange stuff too."

I slide my phone into the pocket of my jeans. "Good to know."

He sits down beside me and fiddles with a leather band on his wrist. "I feel sorry for your roommate."

I frown. "I have a roommate?"

"Everyone new does." He gets to his feet as the conveyer belt buzzes on and reaches for a large duffel bag. "I had one when I first started at the Academy."

"How long have you been going there?" I stand up to grab one of my suitcases.

He slings the bag over his shoulder. "Almost five years."

"So, you're almost nineteen." Disappointment washes over me. "How long do we have to attend the Academy? I thought it was only for a year."

"It all depends on where you're placed. If you want to be a permanent investigator, then you have to put in a lot of time. Otherwise, you'll be put on another job like cleanup, which sucks balls."

"It sounds like it sucks balls." I internally cringe at the idea of having to clean up dead, mangled bodies. "Is that what you do? I mean, are you an investigator?"

"I'm not one yet. I actually took a little time off." He frowns at that then quickly clears his throat. "But, yeah,

I'm back now, and I'm working my way up to becoming an investigator … starting with training you." He motions at me to follow him as he strides for the exit doors.

I totally notice how he breezed over my question about him being at the Black Dungeon. He may think I'm going to drop this, but he's so wrong.

"Training me?" I quickly hurry after him as he exits the building. "I thought we were partners."

"I just said that in front of your dad to make him feel better about the situation." His gaze sweeps the road in front of us and the carport to our right before he veers left down the sidewalk. "I know how proud Keepers need to feel, and it seemed like he'd be prouder if I told him you were my partner."

I wheel my bags with me as we hike toward a black car parked near the curb. "So, I'm not your partner, then."

"Technically, I guess you are, but it's not the same as if you'd actually graduated and are an investigator. I mean, you'll go on jobs with me and everything, but only to learn how we work."

"Sounds like a blast," I say flatly, jerking on my suitcases when a wheel gets stuck in a pothole.

He rounds the back of black car and pats the trunk. Moments later, it pops open. "Doing what we do takes a lot of mental work, Alana." He drops his bag into the trunk then grabs mine from me. "It's not just learning how to fight and jumping in. You have to memorize every creature, learn their traits, what makes them tick so that, when you show up at a crime scene, you'll know what to look for."

Something dawns on me then. Jax knows a lot about creatures. Perhaps he knows what electi means or is.

He heaves my suitcases into the trunk then walks to the side of the car, tipping his head back to glimpse at the sliver of moon in the sky. "Climb in. We have about an hour's drive to the Academy."

I open the door to get into the backseat of the car. "Hey, Jax, can I ask you a question?"

He casts me a wary look from over the car roof. "You can ask, but it doesn't necessarily mean I'll answer."

Sighing, I ask, "Have you ever heard the term electi?"

"Why?"

"I just heard the word once, and didn't know if it meant something or if it was something," I answer as nonchalantly as I can. "You just mentioned how much a Guardian has to learn about the creatures we're hunting, so I figured I'd ask and see if you knew."

"How do you know it's a creature?"

"It's just a guess."

"Well, you guessed wrong, and if I were you, I'd forget the word." He ducks into the backseat of the car and slams the door.

I shake my head. What is with everyone making threats? I've been a part of the Guardians' world for not even twenty–four hours and have been warned twice to keep my mouth shut about stuff. Is this what it's going to be like for the next year? God, I hope not. I've never been one to just drop stuff.

Heaving a sigh, I slide into the backseat. Once I get my seatbelt buckled, the driver, an older man with startling silver hair, drives forward, starting the beginning of a very long and awkward car ride.

Jax is clearly upset with me and decides to do the brooding, silent-guy thing. I try to distract myself with my phone, but the farther into the hills we get, the shittier the signal becomes.

After about half an hour of mind-numbing silence, I scoot forward and prop my arm onto the console. "I just want to say that you have amazing driving skills, dude. Back there, when you took that corner at sixty, that was impressive."

He presses back a smile. "I'm just doing my job,

ma'am. I'm under the instruction to get you to the Academy by eleven-thirty, and not a minute later."

"What happens if I'm late?" I ask curiously.

"Then I lose my job," he replies, shifting gears.

"That's crazy," I say. "I mean, what's the big deal if I'm a few minutes late?"

He shrugs, gripping the wheel. "That's just how things work around there. The Guardians like everything to run in a timely manner."

"Then they're not going to like me very much." I rest my chin on my fist. "I'm always at least five minutes late for everything. Call it a curse. Call it laziness. But I can't seem to break the habit."

"By the end of training, you will," Jax interrupts. "Either that, or you won't make it to the end of training."

I twist around to look at him. "Why? Are they going to kick me out for being late?"

"It's been known to happen a few times."

"Well, then, I'll make sure to be late all the time."

"You act like you want to get kicked out."

"I just want to go home"—I lift my shoulders—"and back to my life."

He slides forward in the seat, getting so close to me his knee presses against my hip. "I know you don't want to hear this, but that isn't your life anymore. The Academy is."

"I never asked for this life. I was supposed to be a Keeper. That's the life I was always planning on having, so it's going to take some time to get used to this whole Guardian thing."

"You need to get over it. You belong to the Guardians now."

I open my mouth to tell him I belong to no one, but snap my jaw shut as the car enters a gated area surrounding a red brick building that seems to stretch for miles.

"It's different than what I expected," I say as the head-lights cast across flowers trimming the dirt driveway and a 'Welcome, New Students' banner above thick double doors at the front of the building. "It's less we-study-dead-bodies-in-here and more hey-come-on-in-and-have-a-cup-of-tea."

"It's a school, Alana, not a mortuary." Jax opens the door as the cars comes to a stop. "We don't study dead bodies in here." He lowers his head to hop out, throwing a smirk over his shoulder at me. "We'll be doing that in the building by the cemetery out back. We use that place so we can run the temperature low to keep the bodies nice and fresh without freezing out the school."

I scrunch my face in disgust, and he chuckles as he

hops out of the car, leaving me to wonder if he was kidding or not.

After we collect our bags from the trunk, I say good-bye to the driver then follow Jax inside the school.

"It's quiet in here," I remark as we walk down a desolate hallway lined with glass cases.

"That's because you're one of the first to arrive." He takes out his phone and glances at the screen before putting it away again.

I notice that inside the cases are tons of framed newspaper clippings with headlines about solved murders. "What newspapers are those from?" I wonder. "Not any from the human world, right?"

"Like the Keepers, humans know nothing of our existence," Jax says as he pulls open a heavy door at the end of the hallway. On the other side of the door is another long hallway lined with more doors.

Jax lets me walk in first then swiftly takes off like a man on a mission. I haul my suitcases behind me as I trudge along behind him. We pass shut door after shut door and finally stop in front of the second to the last one labeled Avery/Clarkford.

"Your roommate won't be here until probably Monday." He drops his bag on the black and white checkered floor and reaches toward me.

Startled, I step away from him. He gives me an annoyed look and grabs ahold of my arm. As his fingers wrap around my wrist, I shiver again from his touch then shake my head at my reaction. What the hell is wrong with me? Seriously, it's not like a guy has never touched me before. I've kissed a few even.

"Why're you trying to hold hands with me?" I ask. "I mean, you're cute and everything, but you're too brooding for my taste."

I feel like an idiot when he flattens my palm against a small pad above the doorknob. The pad lights up, and then the door lock clicks open. He lets go of my hand, gathers his bag, and backs down the hallway.

"We both know I fit your taste. It's why you keep flirting with me."

"I've never flirted with you," I argue, but he simply chuckles and turns his back on me.

Well done, Alana. Never call a cocky guy cute. Now he's never going to let it go.

I blow out a breath before pushing the door open and stepping inside the dark room. Flipping on the light, I see that the room consists of two wooden dressers, two twin metal beds, and a small window.

"This room is so ... depressing," I say to myself as I close the door.

I don't bother unpacking, and sit down on the bed to text Jayse and my grandpa. When none of them answer right away, I lie down, crossing my fingers that I can fall asleep soon. Part of me is hopeful my grandpa Lucas will pay me a visit in my dreams again. Then maybe I can ask him what the hell electi means. That is, if he learned to dream walk. Maybe the damn thing was just a dream. My mind has other ideas, though.

The moment I rest my head on the pillow, my senses are buzzing, my thoughts racing. By the time I doze off, the sun is rising over the hill, and I end up falling into a very disorienting sleep, but I manage to catch a few bits and pieces of the dream.

"Please, Alana," my grandpa pleads. "Please, don't let them find it, even after I'm gone. Keep it safe. It's why I gave it to you: because I know it's safer with you than any-where else."

Chapter 10

A couple of hours after falling asleep, I'm awakened by a godawful buzzing noise.

"Time to get up, Alana." The woman's voice that crackles through the intercom sounds like Vivianne. "You have an orientation tour with a guide in thirty minutes. If you're late, I won't hesitate to put you in detention."

Grumbling, I throw the blankets off me and force my ass out of bed. Faint memories of my grandpa Lucas begging me to keep something he gave me safe echo in my thoughts. The only thing I have with me from him is the dagger. While I still don't know if the dream was real, I'm paranoid enough that I take the dagger out of my suitcases and hide it above a ceiling tile.

After I put the tile back into place, I pull on a pair of shorts, a black tank top, and tie a plaid shirt around my waist. Then I side braid my hair, slip on my boots, and head out to see the place that will be my new home for the next year.

Halfway through the tour, I actually find myself missing Jax, mostly because my tour guide is a cranky old woman who reeks of whiskey. Worse still, every time I ask a question or crack a joke, she looks like she wants to beat me with her cane.

"I don't get why you're asking so many questions," she says when we reach the door to the backyard of the school. "Normally, kids just stand there and listen or text on their phones."

We've walked in so many directions, seen so many classrooms, offices, and libraries that I can't remember which way is left or right or even up and down. I'm all sorts of turned around to the point where I feel like my head is on backward.

"I just want to learn about stuff." I slip on my sunglasses as we step outside and into the sunlight.

Since it's the beginning of August, the temperature is well into the nineties and humid, making it perfect shorts and tank top weather.

As the guide begins a droning story about a stone bench near the fence line, I decide to take her advice and check my text messages. I still haven't heard from my grandpa Lucas or Jayse, even though I messaged them both last night. I have a message from my mom, though.

Mom: Hey, sweetie, just wondering how your first day is going.

Me: I'm just getting a tour. Classes haven't even started yet. In fact, I'm pretty much the only one here right now. Most of the people won't be here until Monday when school officially starts.

Mom: It might be a good thing you're a little bit early. You'll get to learn where everything is before everyone gets there.

Me: I guess so. I just don't get why I couldn't have spent an extra couple of days there with you guys.

Mom: Grandpa thought it'd be best if you got there a little bit early.

Me: Yeah, he's been acting really weird the last couple of days, though. He's not by chance there with you right now, is he? I texted him last night, but he didn't answer.

Mom: He's actually in the City of Crystal for a couple of days, so he might not respond for a bit.

Me: What's he doing there?

Mom: The Foreseers had an emergency meeting about something.

Me: They've been having a lot of meetings lately.

Mom: Sometimes that happens, but I'll make sure

to tell him to message you as soon as he gets back.

Me: Thanks. And tell Jayse the same thing. I haven't heard from him, either.

When she doesn't reply right away, I start to get a little worried something's wrong. What if something happened to Jayse? It makes me hate being so far away and out of the loop.

Me: Is everything okay?

Mom: Yeah, sorry, your father needed help with the grill, and by help, I mean help putting out the fire.

I giggle as I reply.

Me: Dad and his awesome cooking skills. I'm going to miss that.

Mom: You say that now, but when you haven't eaten one of his infamous charred burgers in a few months, you'll be singing another tune.

Me: No way. I'll miss everything, including the burned burgers.

Again, she doesn't text back right away, and I start to feel all those miles between us.

Mom: Hey, honey, I really need to go help your dad before he burns the house down. Call you tonight?

Me: Yes, please. Can I ask you just one more thing, though? It's kind of important.

Mom: Sure.

Me: Has grandpa ever dream walked?

It takes her a moment to respond.

Mom: Why do you ask?

Me: I thought I dreamed about him last night, but it felt real.

Mom: I doubt it was him since Foreseers banned dream walking a long time ago, but I can ask him when he gets in. What exactly happened?

Me: He warned me of danger coming. It was actually very ominous. It's why I asked. I just want to make sure everything's okay with him.

Mom: I'm sure it was probably just a dream, but I'll try to get ahold of him and call u tonight, but u know how hard it is when he's in the city.

Me: Thanks. Oh, and Mom, have you ever heard of the term electi.

Mom: Maybe, but I can't think of what it is off the top of my head. I can look into, though. Was that part of your dream, too?

Me: Yeah, Grandpa said it to me. I don't know what it means, though.

Mom: Look at you, already trying to solve a mystery.

Me: Ha ha, not a murder mystery, though. Just crazy, old grandpa stuff.

Mom: I'll look into everything and call u tonight, okay?

Me: Okay. Thanks, Mom.

Mom: You're welcome, sweetie. And luv u.

Me: Luv u, too.

I put the phone into the pocket of my shorts and lolly-gag behind the tour guide as she leads me toward a cemetery. So, Jax wasn't lying about that. It makes me wonder if he was joking about a building being back here that holds dead bodies.

"This is where we bury most of the Guardians." The guide retrieves a silver flask from her shirt pocket, twists the lid off, and then shakes the crap out of it. "I need a re-fill. Try to get lost while I'm gone so I can end this tour and go home." She rushes back toward the school before I can get a word out.

I press the tips of my fingers to the brim of my nose, feeling a headache coming on. "Is everyone around here an asshole?"

"Don't take it personally. Guardians are a little on the temperamental side. Call it a curse of the job."

The unexpected sound of Jax's voice causes me to

jump.

He's standing near the entrance to the cemetery, leaning against the iron gate, dressed in black jeans with his hoodie pulled over his head.

"Is that why you're so pissy all the time?" I ask, hiking through the grass toward him.

He presses his hand to his chest, pretending to be offended. "I'm never pissy. In fact, I'm quite the opposite."

"Ha, yeah right." I stop just short of him. "Cranky's your middle name."

His lips tip into a playful smile. "No way. My middle name is definitely charmingly adorable."

"More like charmingly pissy."

He chuckles, straightening his stance. "While I'm completely enjoying this flirtatious argument—with a very beautiful girl, I might add—I'm curious why you think I'm an asshole."

"Um, where should I start?" I thrum my finger against my lips. "You've been cranky pretty much since we first met. Well, except for when you gave me the Otium. That was actually a very nice thing to do."

He muses over something as his gaze sweeps up and down my body. I hate to admit it, but my heart rate increases from the attention, my pulse throbbing in the strangest of places and weirdest of ways.

"Tell me"—he steps toward me, closing the distance between us—"besides insulting you, have I done anything else?" He smells differently than he normally does, less like a wolf and more like cologne with a dash of something sugary. He reaches out and ravels a strand of my hair around his finger while staring at my lips. "Like say, have we kissed? I doubt it since I'm so uptight, but you just might be too beautiful for me to resist wanting a taste."

My shock promptly shifts to confusion. "Huh?"

"Leave her alone, Dash." A familiar voice sails over my shoulder.

I whirl around to find Jax striding across the grass toward us with his hands shoved in the pocket of his jeans, his silver eyes gleaming with anger.

"What the hell?" I reel back around to the guy Jax called Dash and narrow my eyes at him.

He looks guilty. "Sorry. I was just curious."

"About what?" I fold my arms and raise my brows, waiting for him to reply.

He opens his mouth to say something, but Jax cuts him off.

"You're not supposed to bother any of the new students," he growls at Dash.

"I wasn't bothering her," Dash replies innocently. "We were just having a nice, little conversation about you and why she thinks you're such a douchebag."

I glance back and forth between the two guys. They're equal height and have the same lean body type, and their facial features are strikingly similar.

"Are you …?" My gaze flicks between them. "Are one of you a doppelganger?"

Jax grinds his teeth. "No, although it might be easier if he was. Then I'd have an excuse every time he fucked up and acted like an ass." Jax glares at Dash then reaches around me and tugs the hoodie off his head. "Alana, meet Dash, my very annoying twin brother."

With the hoodie off, I can see the difference in the two of them. While Jax's hair is light brown and styled in a fauxhawk, Dash's is much darker and cut way shorter. And, unlike Jax's silver eyes, only one of Dash's is silver, while the other is a vibrant shade of teal.

"Twin brother, huh?" I say to Jax. "You couldn't have mentioned that earlier?"

"I was hoping he'd decide not to come here this year." He glares at his brother. "But apparently, he decided to go against our father's wishes."

"Dad has no say in what I do," Dash quips lightly.

"Besides, someone has to watch out for you and make sure you don't work yourself to death."

Jax argues, "I don't work myself to death. It's called being responsible."

"It's called being whipped by our father." Dash tries to make a cracking whip sound that ends up sounding more like an angry cat.

I bite down on my lip, choking on a laugh.

Jax's intense gaze lands on me. "Don't laugh at him. It'll only encourage him. "

I shrug. "Sorry, but the crazy-cat whip sound was kinda, sorta funny."

Dash drapes an arm around my shoulder, and I'm engulfed by the scent of sugar cookies. "See? She thinks I'm funny. You would, too, if Dad didn't have you so brainwashed."

Jax continues to stare at me, seeming almost disappointed. "I'm supposed to take you out with me today, so grab your stuff and meet me out front in twenty."

I want to ask him where we're going, what we're doing, and why he seems so annoyed with his brother, but I don't want to escalate his irritation, especially if I have to spend the entire day with him.

"What about the rest of my tour?" I ask.

"You can finish it later," he says.

I step out from Dash's arm. "It was nice meeting you, Dash." I wave at him as I walk back toward the school. "I'm sure I'll see you later." When Jax's cold eyes land on me, I add, "Maybe."

"Oh, we'll meet again, lovely girl," Dash calls out with a promising grin. "You're far too pretty for me to leave alone."

I snort a laugh, spinning on my heels. As I hurry across the grass, I hear Jax chewing Dash out. I can't hear everything, but I do manage to catch him say, "What are you doing? You know better than to talk to her."

It makes me wonder if he's trying to keep Dash away from me or the other way around.

Chapter 11

"Where are we going?" I ask Jax after we climb into his car, a blue and black striped 1967 Pontiac GTO.

"To the morgue," he says as he steers the car down the dirt drive and toward the main road.

"Seriously?" I cringe when he nods. "So, there's not a building out back of the school that you guys put dead bodies in?"

"No, there is." He flips the visor down as we pull farther away from the trees and school, and sunlight pours into the cab. "But most of the bodies kept there are for class lessons." He casts a sideways glance at me. "Would you chill out? It might seem gross, but you'll get used to it eventually."

I shake my head. "Yeah, I don't think that's ever going to happen."

"Never Giving Up" by Of Mice & Men plays from the stereo, filling the silence between us.

"I don't get you," he finally says. "You come from a

family of Keepers, so I'm sure you've seen dead bodies before. You were also at the Black Dungeon to kill Anastasiya, which would've required you to see her dead if you'd gone through with it. I know you saw her right after she fell off the roof, too, at least that's what the report said."

"Anastasiya would've been my first kill," I admit shamefully, shrugging when he gapes at me. "I've gone on missions a couple of times, but for the most part, my parents don't like me getting involved. They were always too worried that, without being marked, I'd end up getting myself killed. They didn't give me credit, though. I mean, I know I'm not super strong like them or anything, but I can hold my own in a fight. That was kind of the point of killing Anastasiya. I wanted to show them how kickass I was—am." I sigh. "I wasn't going to do it. My friend had already talked me out of it before you decided to threaten me."

"I did that for your own good and to be absolutely certain you didn't go through with it." He slows down the car as we near a sign that reads: Welcome to Maple Spring Valley. "Anastasiya would've snapped your neck like a twig the moment you stepped foot on that roof."

"Yeah, I'm not buying it. I think there's more to it than that."

He cracks his knuckles against the wheel. "Think what you want. I know the truth, and that's all that matters."

I check my phone messages for about the tenth time today, disappointed when I see no new messages. "Why does the Academy even care about someone like Anastasiya? She killed at least a hundred people while she was alive."

Jax heaves a heavy sigh. "Just because she killed people, it doesn't mean we don't need to look into her murder. Every murder case, even when a Keeper kills someone, needs to be investigated so we can keep an eye on things, make sure things don't get out of hand."

"What exactly do you mean by get out of hand?"

"Say whoever killed Anastasiya was part of a bigger plan to take out all the vampires, including ones who haven't killed a single person in their lifetime. If we found out who the person was, we could end up saving innocent lives."

"You consider vampires innocent?"

"Ones who've never killed anyone are innocent, no matter what you've been raised to believe," he says coldly. "Sometimes, innocent people have shitty things happen to them that they wish never happened, but they can't change it." He parks the car in front of a quaint souvenir store located on the corner of a small shopping center. "But they do their best to make good out of a crappy situation."

I swallow hard, feeling like the biggest jerk ever. While I'm not one hundred percent sure that Jax wasn't involved in Anastasiya death, I don't want him to think I believe he's a monster.

"I didn't mean that all vampires are evil. I've just never heard anyone refer to them as innocent."

"That's because you've lived in a world where you assassinate first and investigate later." He removes the keys from the ignition and shoves open the door. "Now, can we please drop this subject? Anastasiya's murder is still an open case, and I've spent so much time reading over her files that I've started to have nightmares about it." He doesn't wait for me to answer before getting out of the car.

I hop out and meet him at the front of the car, staring at the souvenir store. "I thought we were going to a morgue."

"We are." Yawning, he stretches his arms. "The morgue is hidden in back of the store."

I get a brief glimpse of the muscles hidden under his T-shirt, and I can't help gawking. Okay, maybe I was lying when I said he wasn't my type. Personality-wise, not at all, but physically … Well, all I want to do is reach over and trace my fingers along his lean muscles.

When he catches me ogling him, I expect him to throw it in my face, but surprisingly, he leans back against the hood and cocks a questioning brow at me.

I turn my head and roll my eyes at myself. "Why do you bother hiding the morgue? It's not like people are going to steal the bodies."

"It actually happens a lot." He steps away from the car and onto the curb, heading for the store. "We've had to move the location several times to keep thieves from sneaking in."

I follow him to the entrance door. "Why would anyone want to steal a dead body?"

"For a lot of reasons." A bell dings as he pulls open a door. He holds it open for me, letting me step in first. "Think about the powerful things that come through here," he says as the door swings shut behind us. "Warlocks, Pixies, Faeries. We even had a Nymph once, and you know how wanted their blood is. There's an entire black market centering on just that."

"Okay, I guess I see your point, but it's still gross." I glance around at the shelves on the wall carrying knick-knacks, T-shirts, maps, and every other kind of souvenir a tourist could ever dream of. "So, where's this hidden morgue?"

Entranced

Jax grins at me as he rounds the back of the front counter, gesturing for me to follow him as he ducks through a beaded curtain. I step through the curtain and into a backroom full of rows and rows of bookshelves angled in every direction.

"God, it's like a maze in here …" I trail off. "Jax?" I inch forward toward the shelves. "Jax, I didn't see where you—"

A solid chest presses against my back as warm hand covers my mouth. Seconds later, I'm pulled backward. I expect us to hit the wall, but somehow, we disappear *into* the wall. I freak the fuck out for two point five seconds, preparing to attack, until I get a whiff of Jax's wolf scent. Even though I'm not going to let him off the hook for the move, I simmer my attack down, not wanting to hurt him.

At least not too badly, anyway.

Grabbing his wrist, I lightly twist and pull while bringing my foot up and nudging him back. Startled, he quickly pulls away.

"Dude, what's up with the surprise attack?" I ask, putting my hands on my hips.

"I was trying to get you inside without having to show you how to get in … I'm technically not allowed to show you just yet." He rubs his wrists, chuckling softly. "Fuck, you're a lot stronger than you look."

"Remember that the next time you try to grab me from behind," I say with a smirk.

He smashes his lips together, trying hard to muffle a laugh.

I bite back a smile. "Quit being a perv."

"You're the one who said it." He lowers his hand to his side, and we stand there like idiots, grinning goofily at each other.

A couple of days ago, I thought I'd never have fun again. And while this isn't the spending-an-entire-day-hunting-a-vampire kind of fun, I'm not gouging my eyes out from boredom like I thought I would.

Maybe this whole Guardian thing might not be so bad after all.

Right as the thought crosses my mind, I become hyperaware of the cold air seeping into my skin. I skim the metal walls around me, realizing we're by the mortuary cold chambers.

I scrunch up my nose. "So, this is where the magic happens?"

"Not really." Jax's rolls up the sleeves of his hooded shirt, grabs a hand of one of the middle section chambers, and pulls it open, sliding out a bulky body bag. "If you end up being an investigator, you probably won't spend a lot of time in here. You'll mostly go to the scenes"—he reaches for the zipper of the body bag while I fight back a gag—"to interview witnesses and go through a lot of fucking paperwork. Sometimes, you'll have to come here to check on some of the facts, though."

I cover my mouth with my hand as he unzips the bag. The stench hits me before he even gets it all the way open, like rotting eggs and vomit. "What the hell's in there?"

"A Zombie," he says, looking completely unbothered by the stench.

"It smells horrible. Like—"

"Like rotting death?" He glances at me with amusement dancing in his eyes. "You'll get used to it."

"You keep saying that."

"That's because it's true." He leans over the Zombie, inspecting the rotting flesh peeling away from the once human face. "A lot of Guardians are like you when they first start." His forehead creases as he studies the left cheek of the zombie's face. "Being around death is in your blood even if you think it isn't; otherwise, you wouldn't have gotten the mark."

I absentmindedly touch the mark on the back of my neck. "How many people in your family are Guardians?"

"My parents both are and so is my sister," he says, brushing his hair out of his eyes as he leans in closer to the zombie. "Dash... He's one, too, but he's ..." He trails off, clearing his throat. "Well, he's a little less invested in the job than my family is."

I want to ask him if Dash is something other than just a Guardian. I don't know why I think he might be other than the odd sugary scent coming off him. I don't know of any creatures who smell like sugar other than Sprites, but that's because they have sweet tooths. Dash can't be a Sprite, though, since they don't take on human form.

Before I can ask Jax about it, he motions me to come over to him.

I inch back. "No thanks. I'm good right here."

He gives me a tolerant look. "Alana, I just want to show you something. I promise you don't have to touch it."

I begrudgingly inch over beside him, rubbing my nose as the stench burns at my nostrils.

"See this right here?" He points at a faint sequence of symbols carved on the Zombie's left cheek.

I nod. "It looks like a tag for a paranormal experimental facility."

I try not to shudder. Paranormal experimental facilities are the worse. They kidnap anything with magic in their blood, including Keepers, lock them up, and do all sorts of experiments on them.

His brows furrow. "How do you know about tags?"

I shrug. "My parents talk about it sometimes. It's crazy how many paranormal experiment facilities they've had to tear down."

"Yeah, they're on the rise, too."

"Really?"

He nods, reaching to zip up the bag. "I've been noticing a lot of tags lately." After he zips up the bag, he pushes it back into the chamber. "And not just on Zombies. On Vampires, Fey," his voice drops a notch, "Wolves." He clears his throat. "But anyway, I've been looking into it, and I think they might be linked to each other somehow. I just don't know who's running the show."

"Is that part of your job?" I ask with skepticism. "To find out who's tagging?"

"I told you there was more to our job than finding dead bodies." He steps toward me, tugging the sleeves of his shirt down. "Now, close your eyes."

I eye him with distrust. "Why?"

He gives me a blank stare. "Because I'm going to shove you in the body bag with the Zombie." When I roll my eyes, his lips quirk. "I need you to shut your eyes so I can get us out of here without you seeing where the entrance and exit to this room is."

"Fine." I heave a dramatic sigh, pretending it's a bigger deal than it is.

Once I get my eyes shut, he steers me somewhere with his fingers enclosed around my upper arms and his chest pressed against my back. I try to breathe normally, but for some reason, my breathing is coming out in sharp, uneven pants. It only becomes harder to get air into my lungs when he moves his hands to my waist, his fingers brushing against my bare skin.

I feel like I should say something, remind him of my no-touching rule. I mean, we just got all up in a Zombie for God's sake. I shouldn't want him touching me.

But it kinda feels nice.

Okay, a lot nice.

Thank God he finally comes to a stop; otherwise, I might have done something stupid, like said my thoughts aloud or touched him back. Considering he's my teacher or whatever the hell his title is—I'm still not clear on that—I don't think it'd be wise to get involved with him.

His fingers tense for a brief second before they fall from my waist. I take a deep breath and open my eyes, sighing in relief when I see that I'm standing in the center of the souvenir store again. I breathe in the fresh scent of non-Zombie air, smiling, glad to be out of the morgue. But when I catch sight of Jax staring at his phone, his skin as pale as a ghost, my smile falters.

"What's wrong?" I ask. "Why do you look like... well, like you just examined a dead Zombie?"

He blinks up at me, paling even more. "We need to go back to the Academy."

"Did something happen?"

"We ... I got called in on a case." His Adam's apple bobs up and down as he swallows hard. "Alana, the name listed on the case file is ... It's Julian Lucas."

Chapter 12

Jax starts explaining to me what happened, but I'm in too much shock, and I barely hear anything he says.

My grandpa Lucas is dead?

My grandpa Lucas was murdered?

Oh, my God. I'm never going to see him again.

I wrap my arm around my stomach as tears pour out of my eyes.

Jax grows quiet after that and guides me to the car. He hardly says anything to me during the drive back to the Academy, letting me cry to myself. I keep thinking about my dream and how worried he sounded, how worried he looked the day before I left. I knew something was wrong, and I didn't do anything about it.

I should have done something.

I should have helped him.

"It's going to be okay," Jax says after he parks the car in the garage adjacent to the Academy.

"Do my ...? Do my parents know yet?" I choke

through the tears.

"I'm not sure," he says. "A Guardian should be heading over to their house to tell them, but it might take a bit …" He seems unsure about something. "You can call them, though … if you want to."

My eyes pool with tears as I nod and get out of the car.

We walk in silence as we cross the dirt drive and head into the school. All I want to do is go to my room, call my mom and dad, and cry my eyes out, but Jax gently touches my arm, stopping me.

"I know you probably want to go to your room," he says in an apologetic tone, "but I'm supposed to take you to Vivianne's office first."

The last thing I want to do is talk to anyone. But I'm too emotionally exhausted to argue, and I easily surrender and follow Jax to Vivianne's office located smack dab in the middle of the maze of hallways.

He knocks on the door then turns to me, seeming apprehensive. "I can wait for you if you need me to."

"I'm fine." My voice sounds so hollow.

He hesitates to leave. "Are you sure? Because I can stick around for a bit. At least until you're done talking to her."

"I'll be fine. Thanks for the offer, though."

With a reluctant look on his face, he heads down the hallway.

As the quietness sets in, my mind turns on. I start thinking of *everything* when all I want to do is think of *nothing*. I almost call Jax back just so he can distract me from the pain, but the door in front of me opens.

Vivianne stands there with her hair pulled into a tight bun and a too-pleasant look on her face. "Alana, please come in."

I wipe my cheeks with my hand before stepping inside her office.

She shuts the door and gestures at a chair in front of a mahogany desk. "Please, have a seat."

When I sink into the chair, she takes a seat at her desk and quietly studies me for a moment.

"You look like him." She says it as if the fact disgusts her.

I ball my hands into fists. "Is that why you brought me in here? Or did you actually have a point?"

Anger flashes in her eyes as she reclines back in her chair, crossing her legs. "You know, I felt a little bit sorry for you when I first heard the news, but now that you're here, displaying that arrogant Keeper attitude, I think part of me is going to enjoy telling you this."

"Telling me what? That my grandpa is dead?" The firmness in my voice cracks. "Because Jax already told me."

Her eyes darken as her lips curl into a smile. "Did he tell you why he was killed?"

I don't know how to respond. He could have told me at some point, and I was just too out of it to hear him.

"Your grandpa was a fugitive and was harboring the Dagger of Conspectu. And by the way your face drained of color, I'm guessing you know what that is." She shifts forward in her seat, looking twistedly pleased by my pain. "You know as well as I do that he wasn't supposed to have that dagger. No one is. That's why it's kept locked up in The Vault."

"I don't know what you're talking about. I've never heard of this dagger or The Vault," I lie in an even tone.

I'm technically not supposed to know what The Vault is, but I accidentally overheard my parents whispering about the place Keepers keep every powerful weapon they accumulate during raids. There are so many weapons the walls are laced with every kind of magic repellant to keep anyone from getting inside. If anyone did get their hands on some of the stuff hidden in there, they could pretty much start an apocalypse.

As for the dagger, I've never heard of it before, but I'm pretty sure it's the dagger I have hidden in my bedroom ceiling.

"Are you sure about that?" she says simply. "Because I have a source that says your grandfather might have told you where he put the dagger."

My palms dampen with sweat, but thank God my voice comes out steady. "Why would he tell me that? I'm just his granddaughter."

The darkness in her expression sends a chill up my spine. "He broke the law when he stole the dagger. And anyone who's helped him—who knows where the dagger is and doesn't say anything—can be held accountable for the crime."

My grandfather's words echo in my mind.

"Please, Alana," my grandpa pleads. "Please, don't let them find it, even after I'm gone. Keep it safe. It's why I gave it to you: because I know it's safer with you than any-where else."

Whether it was a dream or not, I'm not about to tell this woman anything, not until I find out what's going on, who *they* are.

"It's a good thing I don't know where it is, then, huh?" My heart hammers in my chest, but I refuse to look away from her.

She looks like she wants to wring my neck. "Don't be stupid, Alana. Your grandfather got himself killed over this, but you can walk out of it just fine. All you need to do is tell me where it is."

"I can't tell you where it is, because I don't know."

Her eyes flash with rage as she balls her hands into fists. "Fine. You can leave, then," she bites out. "But if you change your mind, you know where my office is."

My legs shake as I get up and head for the door.

"And, Alana, you have detention when you return from the funeral, and you'll be spending it in here with me." She sounds elated by the fact.

I glance over my shoulder at her. "What for?"

"For withholding information about a case," she says, opening her desk drawer. "Because I know you know more than you're letting on. It's a gift of mine. I can read when people are lying. It's why I'm the Head of Interrogation."

Grinding my teeth, I open the door and step out of her office. I start down the hallway, planning to run to my room and call my parents, tell them everything that's happened, but I startle when I spot Jax leaning against the wall.

"What are you doing out here?" I ask, wiping my sweaty palms on the sides of my shorts.

He seems unsure about something. "I just wanted to make sure you were okay … I know Vivianne can be a little intense and uncompassionate."

"I can handle Vivianne," I say, "but thanks for checking on me."

"Do you need anything?" He tugs his fingers through his hair. "We can go kick the crap out of a heavy bag or something? It might be a good distraction until we can get you on a flight back home."

"Aren't you supposed to be working on my grandfather's case?" I ask, my voice uneven as tears sting my eyes again. I refuse to cry, though. Not until I get to the bottom of this and clear my grandpa's name.

Vivianne may think he's a thief, but I know my grandpa. If he took the dagger, it was for a good reason.

"I can spare a few hours if you need me to."

"Can I …?" God, I can't believe I'm asking this, but if I'm going to get any answers, this is the best place to start. "Can I go with you?"

His eyes widen. "Go with me where? To the crime scene?"

I nod, swallowing down the nausea burning up my throat. "I want to help find who killed him."

"I'm not sure that's a good idea... Usually, we don't allow people to get involved with cases they are emotionally connected to."

"Please, Jax," I beg. "I need to do something besides sit around or kick the crap out of a bag. I need to feel like I'm helping him."

He deliberates, looking so reluctant I'm positive I'm going to have to get on my knees and beg. Then he shocks the crap out of me when he nods.

"If you want to come with me after everything is cleaned up and you return back to school, then you can, but if at any time it looks like you're about to fall apart, you're off the case."

I suck in a breath. Cleaned up? Like my grandpa's body?

"O-okay, that sounds fair."

"You should go pack your stuff," he says as we walk down the hall. "I just informed Ms. Fellingford, the secretary, and she's trying to get you on a flight back home ASAP."

I nod and thank him again, even giving him a hug. At first, he's stiff when I wrap my arms around him, but he eventually loosens up and slips an arm around me.

"Thanks for your help … and making sure I'm okay." Tears burn in my eyes as I quickly move back and hurry to my room.

I immediately try to call my mom and then my dad, but neither of them answer their phones. Either they're on a mission, or a Guardian is at the house, breaking the news to them.

I call Jayse, needing to talk to someone, anyone from back home, but he doesn't answer, either.

"Where are you?" I say to his voicemail. "I've tried to call you, like, twenty times ... Something bad happened, Jayse. I need you. Please call me back."

Dazedly, I start to pack my suitcase, stuffing my clothes inside. Then I lock the door and check around the room before I slide the ceiling tile out of the way and retrieve the dagger.

I don't know what it does or why my grandpa was hiding it, but I'm not about to leave it here for someone to find it while I'm gone. I'm going to protect it with my life until I figure out what the hell is going on.

Chapter 13

Growing up as part of the Keepers circle, death happened often, but it never hit so close to home until I lost my grandpa.

Death is brutal. Death is painful. Death makes you think of all the things you wished you'd done and said yet can never say or do again. Death, the end of someone's life and the beginning of your life without them. Death is overwhelming to take in, which is why I'm currently and purposefully living in denial.

I've been home from the Academy for four days and haven't shed a single tear. I distract my pain with hours of kickboxing, fencing, and self-defense lessons. I know I'm overworking myself, but the moment I stop, the pain will hit me like a violent wave. Eventually, I'll have to stop and feel the pain, but not yet. I just need a little more time to breathe.

My mom, on the other hand, has been crying for days. My dad and I constantly try to comfort her, but she always stops crying the second we try to console her and makes up an excuse of something she needs to do, like the dishes, and hastily leaves the room.

"I'm worried about her," I announce to my dad as I wander into the living room and slump into a chair across from him

He removes his attention from the sword he's sharpening and looks up at me. "It'll just take some time, Alana. She'll be okay eventually. Your mom's strong."

I rest back, exhausted. "I just wish she'd talk to someone. She's barely said anything since I got home."

"She talks to me every night." He sets the sword on the coffee table. "I think she's just being cautious around you."

I pull my long, brown hair into a ponytail and secure it with an elastic. "Why? I'm fine."

"You are, huh?" He eyes over my yoga pants, sneakers, and tank top that reek of sweat. "Then what's with the crazy work-outs?"

I shrug, picking at the midnight blue polish on my fingernails. "I thought I'd take advantage of it before I go back to the Academy and trade my strength for brainpower."

He frowns. "I can tell when you're lying."

I grimace. "Fine. Keeping busy, working out … It distracts me, okay?"

His expression softens. "I know you miss your grandpa. The two of you were close, but sooner or later you're going to have to deal with this."

"I'm not ready to deal with it yet ..." I suck back the tears burning in my eyes and spring from the chair. "I'm going to go see if Jayse is home."

He opens his mouth to call me back, but I'm already rushing out the front door.

Clouds grumble in the sky, promising rain, as I jog across the dry field and toward Jayse's house. I send him a text on my way, hoping he's made it home by now.

After I found out about my grandpa's death, I messaged him for three days straight without getting a response. He finally replied last night and told me he was up in the mountains where he barely got a signal, but that he'd be home today. I haven't heard from him since then, and I'm growing worried he won't be back in time for the funeral tonight.

A thought creeps into the back of my mind. *What if Jayse is blowing me off on purpose?* The Keepers have been acting very standoffish since my Grandpa Lucas was accused of stealing the Dagger of Conspectu. My mom and dad have been arguing his innocence with everyone, and I haven't had the heart to tell them that I currently have the dagger hidden in my room because Grandpa asked me to hide it.

I shake my head at my thoughts and try to reassure myself aloud. "No, Jayse will make it to the funeral. He's my best friend."

When I reach the flattened area of the field, I quicken my pace. Nearing the property line, the clouds make good on their promise, and rain showers down from the sky.

As raindrops splatter against my skin, I remember the first time my grandpa took me archery shooting. I was six years old and didn't even know how to hold the bow.

"Now carefully lift it up," he said, "until the tip of the arrow is pointing at the target."

"What color do I want to hit?" I asked, squinting at the target.

"The red."

"The red …? But it's so small. It's gonna be super hard to hit it."

"That's kind of the point. It wouldn't be challenging if it were easy. And you don't have to hit the red. Let's just work on getting the arrow shooting forward, okay?"

I nodded, pulled back the string, and let the arrow spring forward. It went about five feet before nose-diving into the dirt.

He chuckled and told me that it was okay, that I should be proud of myself for making it that far. Then he had me try again, and I failed at least fifty times. It had started raining by then, but I refused to go inside until I made it on the target.

"I have to do it, Grandpa," I said determinedly. "Just one time. Then I'll go inside."

"Oh, fine," he sighed, but a smile lit up his violet eyes. "But if your parents ask, we went inside the second it started to rain."

I nodded, and he stood with me until I managed to make it on the target. He never grew frustrated or rushed me. He was happy to see me so motivated, and because of him, I became fantastic at archery.

God, I miss him so, so much.

By the time I reach the porch of the Hale's home, the rain has soaked through my clothes.

I rap my hand on the door before rushing inside.

"Alana, honey, what's going on?" my aunt Aislin says as I stumble into the living room, shivering from the cold, my nerves, *everything*.

"Is Jayse here?" I ask through my chattering.

She rises from the chair she's sitting in and rushes over

to me. "He hasn't made it home yet, but I can try to call him and see where he is."

I wipe raindrops from my cheeks with the sleeve of my shirt. "I just tried to message him, and he didn't answer."

"He might be in the middle of traveling, or he hasn't gotten out of the mountains yet. I'm sure he'll be here … He has to." But she seems worried that he might not.

"Where is he exactly?" I ask, hugging my arms around myself.

She presses her lips together, wavering. "Oh, I'm not quite sure. Somewhere … in the mountains."

As a boom echoes from somewhere in the house, she tenses.

She's being too evasive. Something odd's going on.

"What was that?" I ask, watching her reaction closely.

"Nothing," she says, being all twitchy.

"Where's Uncle Laylen?" I peer over my shoulder at the stairway then at the kitchen to my right before locking my gaze on her.

"He, um…" She fidgets with her floral dress, smoothing invisible wrinkles from the fabric. "I think he went to pick up Jayse from the airport."

"But you just said you didn't know when Jayse would be home. And since when do Keepers fly on planes?"

Another thud, this time from the basement.

Her eyes widen as I whirl around and hightail it toward the basement door located in the kitchen.

"Alana." She chases after me, her heels clicking against the hardwood floor. "Please, don't go in there."

I stride up to the basement door and wrap my fingers around the doorknob. "Can't you hear that? There's something down there."

"Yes, but it's nothing." She stops beside me. "A cat probably just got in. You know how spacey your uncle Laylen can get. He's always leaving the windows open."

I shoot her a doubtful look. "I guess we better go get it out of there, then."

"Alana, don't," she pleads as I pull open the door.

Buzz ... buzz ... Don't listen to the voices ... Block them out ... Be strong...

"What the hell is that?" I shout, throwing my hands over my ears.

The color drains from Aislin's face as she glances from the basement doorway to me. Her lips move, but I can't tell what she's saying.

Don't listen to the voice ... Don't give in to the cravings ... Fight it ... Fight ...

The world sways as I stumble to the side, my head

throbbing with the sound of the voice.

Jayse suddenly appears in the doorway as the buzzing takes over my thoughts, and he yanks me into the darkness.

Chapter 14

"Alana, did you hide it?" my grandpa asks through the haziness funneling around me. "Did you hide the dagger?"

"I have it ... in my room ... I didn't want to leave it at the Academy." I struggle to open my eyes again, desperate to see him, but my eyelids won't budge.

"Good girl. But I think you should find a better place to hide it. Somewhere safe where no one can find it," he says. "Have you told anyone you have it?"

"I haven't yet ... I was going to tell my mom and dad, but ... Well, my mom's been really upset ever since you died. She's convinced you're innocent. I'm worried, if I tell her you did steal it, she might break apart."

"I'm glad you haven't told her. I don't want her to know about it. Promise me you won't tell her yet, not until my name is cleared."

"But everyone thinks you stole it, and you kind of did, didn't you?" I feel awful for saying it, but I need to understand why he took the dagger. "Everyone's calling you a

thief and a traitor and saying you took it because you were planning to use it for something terrible."

"Do you believe what everyone's saying?"

"No ... but I wish you'd tell me why you took it."

He grows quiet.

I try to open my eyes again, but the damn things won't open. I want to cry. Scream! Let out all the anger and pain I've been keeping trapped inside me.

"Why can't I see you?" I ask in frustration.

"It's better if you don't," he answers simply.

"Why not?"

"Because it'll only make things more complicated." *He sighs. "Alana, I know it's hard, but you have to let me go."*

"But I don't think I can," I whisper. "Every time I think about how you're gone, it feels like I'm going to break apart."

"You're stronger than you give yourself credit. You'll get through this."

Tears burn my eyes. "You've always been overly confident in me."

"Come on; open your eyes. Please, Alana."

"Oh, no, we're running out of time," my grandpa says in a panic. "There's so much more I need to tell you."

Entranced

Consciousness creeps through the cracks in my mind. "Please, Grandpa, tell me why you stole the dagger."

"Because a war is coming ..." His voice drifts farther away.

"What war? The one you were talking about before I left for school?" When he doesn't respond, I beg, "Please, don't leave yet. I'm not ready to let go. I have so many questions. Like what's electi.*" Silence is my only answer. "Grandpa, please!"*

"Electi ... Stay away ... You have to be strong ... to survive the war ..."

Chapter 15

"Alana, wake up!"

Water sprinkles across my face and I jolt awake, gasping for air. The lights sting my eyes, and I blink insanely, trying to adjust to the brightness and regain my bearings.

I'm in Aunt Aislin's kitchen, lying on the tile floor, and Jayse is leaning over me with a cup of water in his hand.

Wait ... Jayse?

"What the hell?" I start to sit up even though I'm dizzy as hell.

"Jesus, you scared the shit out of me." Jayse sits back on his heels, giving me room as he sets the cup of water down on the floor.

I clutch my throbbing head. "What happened?"

He releases a stressed breath as he rakes his fingers through his blond hair. "I think you fainted."

It all rushes back to me: Aunt Aislin freaking out when I tried to open the door, the voice I heard right before I blacked out ...

I glance around the empty kitchen. "Where'd your mom go?"

His gaze flicks to the doorway. "She ... She went upstairs to get some Oriuntur so we could wake you up."

I can tell he's lying. It's written all over his face.

My gaze wanders to the closed basement door. "Something was down there. I heard it ... It told me not to give into my cravings. I'm not sure what I'm craving, but it seemed pretty adamant that I was definitely craving something."

He clenches his jaw. "I'm not sure what you heard, but there's nothing down there."

I sit up straight and rub my eyes with my hands. "Jayse, I know you're lying, so fess up."

His Adam's apple bobs as he swallows hard. "I hate lying to you, but I can't tell you."

"Yes, you can. We've always told each other everything."

"Not this time." His voice is strained. "Please, just let this go."

The fear in his tone sends warning flags popping up all over the place.

My hands fall to my lap. "Are you in some kind of

trouble?"

He hesitates, seeming torn. "I—"

Relief sweeps across his face as his mom enters kitchen, carrying a small bag of dried flower petals.

"Okay, I have a little bit of Oriuntur left ..." She trails off as her gaze lands on me. "Oh, good, you're awake." She drops the bag of dried flower petals onto the table, crouches down in front of me, and flattens her palm to my forehead.

"What are you doing?" I ask as she carefully grabs my wrist, pressing two fingers to my pulse.

"Just making sure your vitals are okay." She counts the beat of my pulse under her breath.

I give Jayse a what-the-hell-is-going-on look, but he avoids eye contact with me.

"I need to take a shower before the funeral." He pushes to his feet. "Do you want to meet me at your house or in the city?"

He's being cold, and I hate it. I've been waiting for him to get home because he can usually cheer me up when I'm having trouble dealing with something. But right now, I feel worse than I did before I fainted.

"Is this because I'm a Guardian?" I stumble to my feet. "Is that why you guys are keeping stuff from me?"

Aislin stands up and nervously glances at Jayse. They

exchange a look before Jayse discreetly shakes his head once.

"No one's keeping anything from you." Jayse's tone is clipped. "So let it go."

I smash my lips together, wrestling back the tears. I can't take this right now. I need my best friend, not this Keeper standing in front of me.

"Fine. I'll see you at the funeral." I brush by him, making a beeline for the front as the pain I've been burying claws its way to the surface.

"Alana," Aislin calls out after me.

Ignoring her, I burst outside. Tears flood my eyes as I run down the porch steps and sprint blindly across the field, rain pouring down on me.

I can't see, think, breathe. I just want to understand why it happened. Why he died. Why he had the dagger. Why? Why? Why?

"Alana!" Jayse shouts from behind me.

I quicken my pace. "Leave me alone!"

"Would you wait just a damn minute!" he yells, his footsteps approaching. "I need to talk to you!"

I try to outrun him, but a second later, he snags ahold of my arm, and I clumsily stumble to a stop.

Damn him and his stupid inhuman Keeper's speed.

I wrench my arm from his grasp and swing around to face him. "What do you want?"

"I ..." He stares at the trees in the distance, massaging the back of his neck tensely. "You're right. I am keeping something from you, but ..." He looks at me, his eyes silently pleading for me to understand. "I can't tell you. I want to, but I ..." He swallows hard. "Please don't be mad at me."

I want to stay mad at him. Being mad at him is easier than being sad, but being sad is becoming too much to endure. I can't hold it in any longer.

A sob wrenches from my chest as I collapse to my knees in the mud. "I just miss him."

"I know you do." He kneels in front of me. "I'm sorry I snapped at you. I've been a shitty best friend lately."

I sniffle. "You haven't been shitty; you've just been ... distracted."

"I know." He doesn't embellish, doesn't argue. He doesn't say that he'll get better. He just sits there in the rain with me while I cry. For a moment, everything feels okay again, like it did when we were kids and life wasn't so complicated. Ultimately, though, the rain stops, my tears dry, and Jayse grows uneasy again.

"I have to go inside." He pushes to his feet. "I'll see

you tonight, okay?"

I nod, wiping my eyes with the back of my hand. He casts me an apologetic look before jogging away, leaving me standing alone in the field.

I watch him leave, worried nothing will be the same between us again.

Chapter 16

When I get home, I race up to my room and change into a pair of dry sweatpants and a tank top. Then I wander into my dad's office to steal a few books about identifying otherworldly creatures and their traits, figuring research can distract me for a bit. I've already read through three books since I came home, searching for any terminology related to electi. So far, though, I've come up with zilch.

"Hey, sweetie," my mom says as we cross paths in the hallway. Her gaze travels to the books in my arms, and a pucker forms at her brows. "Still trying to find information on electi, huh?"

I hug the books to my chest. "It was the last thing Grandpa said to me, and I feel like I should keep looking into it until I find out what it means, even if it ends up being nothing."

A look of understanding crosses her face. "I really wish I'd had a chance to ask him about it before …" She clears her throat, her violet eyes pooling with tears. "Do you need help with anything? Maybe I could talk to a few more Keepers about it." She frowns. "Although, this whole thing with your grandpa and the dagger might make it a little bit complicated to get a straightforward answer from anyone."

I force a smile. "It's okay, Mom. I think I'll stick with the books for now. Besides, I'm not even sure if it's something the Keepers have heard of. It might not even be a creature."

Honestly, the easiest way to get to the bottom of it would be to pry the truth out of Jax with a little bit of torture. But since he's a werewolf/guardian, I'm not so sure my average strength would stand against his freakishly strong wolf skills.

My mom mulls over something while twisting a strand of her long, brown hair around her finger. "Maybe I can ask your grandma if she knows anything about electi and if your grandpa had been dreamwalking." She unravels her hair from her finger, sighing. "I'd like to wait a few days if that's okay, though. She's having a hard time with…" She releases a shaky breath. "Well, you know."

I nod, silently telling the waterworks to back the hell off. The last thing I need is to break down in front of my mom.

I give her a hug. "Thanks, Mom."

She wraps her arms around me, hugging me back. "For what?"

For listening to me. For not lying to me. For caring. For everything. "For being a good mom. I feel like I don't say it enough."

"Thank you for being an amazing daughter." Her arms tremble as she holds me tighter. "I love you, honey."

"I love you, too." I take a few measured breaths before I step back. "You know what? If you really want to help me read through these"—I pat the books in my hand—"I'd totally appreciate it. I love reading and everything, but these books are about as boring as a math textbook."

A ghost of a smile rises on her lips. "I'd love to."

We spend the next couple of hours skimming through each leather-bound book. Around one o'clock, she leaves my room to get ready for the funeral. Since it doesn't start for a few more hours, I remain on my bed, flipping through page after page until my eyes start to burn and the letters bleed together.

"This is useless. There's nothing in here ... Maybe it was just a dream after all ..." I close the book, push it aside, and rest my head on my pillow.

I try to go to sleep, hoping to drift into dreamland

where my grandpa will be waiting with the answers. Then again, the only time he's visited me in my dreams since he died was when I heard that voice at Jayse's and fainted. Perhaps that had something to do with it, but I don't even know what *the voice* was.

I stare at the stack of books beside me, wondering if any of them can help me figure out what the voice was. I instantly scrunch up my nose at the idea of reading more droning knowledge on every creature that's ever walked the earth.

"Man, I need to find a better way to get some answers," I mumble. "There has to be a quicker way to do this …" I glance at my phone on the nightstand.

Hmmm … I could call Jax. He might know something about the voice. And before I left the Academy, he did give me his number and told me I could call him if I needed to. But would he even tell me if he did know something? He did completely refuse to give me answers when I asked him about electi. Then again, it doesn't hurt to try.

I sit up, grab my phone, and dial his number.

"Hello," he picks up after four rings, sounding really confused.

"Um, hey, it's me." As silence fills the line, I add, "Alana … Avery."

"Thanks for adding the last name; otherwise, I'd never have figured out which Alana was calling me. There's so many in my life."

After days and days filled with mourning and crying, his sarcasm is like a breath of fresh air.

"Well, you are a little slow sometimes," I joke, leaning against the headboard, "so I thought I'd make it easy on you."

"How very generous of you," he replies in a light, almost playful tone that sounds oddly out of place for him.

"Did you by chance get taken over by body snatchers while I've been gone?"

"No. Why?"

"Because you sound weirdly happy right now."

"What exactly does weirdly happy sound like?"

"You being happy."

"So, you're saying it's weird when I'm happy?" Amusement rings in his tone.

I stretch out my legs, stifling a yawn. "Yeah. You're usually moody all the time."

"I'm not moody all the time," he argues. "Just most of the time."

"Okay, I'll give you that one."

"Gee, thanks. I feel so special now."

"You're very welcome."

The big, old smile on my face is completely unexpected and kind of makes me feel guilty. Am I supposed to smile yet? It doesn't seem like I should be, especially with how upset my mom looked when she left the room.

And there goes my smile.

"I actually called to ask for a favor," I quickly change the subject before I start crying.

"Okay … What's up?" He seems reluctant.

"It's not a big deal or anything. I just need some info about something that happened today," I say then give him a brief rundown of what happened at Jayse's.

"What did the voice sound like?" he asks after I finish.

I chew on my thumbnail. "Honestly, it sounded kind of robotic, like a recording."

"Maybe it *was* just a recording," he suggests evasively.

"But I didn't hear it outside of my head," I point out. "It was inside my mind."

"Maybe it was your conscious or your second personality," he says amusedly.

I roll my eyes. "Telling me to block out cravings? Because the only cravings I have right now are for chocolate and kickboxing."

"Kickboxing? Really?"

"What? It helps clear my mind, okay?

"Okay." There's a dragged out pause before he speaks again, his tone carrying caution. "How are you doing with everything?"

I frown at the turn of the conversation. "Fine, I guess."

"Good." He sounds as uncomfortable as I feel. "Do you …? Do you need anything?"

I press my lips together and inhale deeply, trying to chill the heck out. "Yeah, for you to tell me what you think that voice could be."

He sighs. "I already told you some ideas, and other than those, I have no idea."

"You know I can tell when you're full of shit, right?"

"Bullshit." His tone carries a hint of amusement mixed with annoyance. "You've only known me for, like, a week. You have no clue if I'm lying or not."

I roll onto my stomach. "Hate to break it to ya, but you're kind of an open book."

He snorts a laugh. "Most people usually say the opposite about me."

"Well, most people don't have mad people reading skills."

"Or maybe you're just trying to play me right now."

"Maybe. Maybe not. Perhaps, I do have you all figured

out."

"No one has me all figured out," he mutters more to himself.

Silence fills the line.

"Fine," he surrenders, and a smile creeps up on my face. "But are you sure you want to know what I think the voice was? Because it's really bad."

His ominous tone sends a chill rippling through my body.

"How bad are we talking?" I ask.

"Like, life changing bad," he replies.

"For me?"

"No, for either your aunt or your cousin. It all depends on who the voice was there for."

I swallow the nausea burning at the back of my throat. Can I take any more bad news? The ache in my chest and the burning in my stomach beg me to hang up without hearing the answer, but I've never been one to run from the truth. Good or bad, I'd rather know than live in a world webbed with lies.

"Tell me what you think it is," I say quietly.

He sighs disappointedly. "A Transition Reprogrammer. They basically help a human make the transition to inhuman."

I gulp. "How exactly does it work?"

"Take, for instance, if someone were bitten by a were-wolf and they wanted to do their best not to give in to the overpowering rage and need to kill. They could have a Transition Re-programmer to help ease the cravings." The edge in his tone makes me wonder if he's used a Transition Re-programmer.

I fiddle with the corner of a book. "This thing, this Transition Re-programmer, is it a creature? Or is it like a computer? Because it sounds like a self-help tape."

He laughs hollowly. "It's definitely more aggressive than a self-help tape."

"So it's a creature?"

"No, not exactly."

"Okay ... I'm so confused."

"It's hard to explain." Silence briefly stretches between us before he continues, "It's kind of like a shadow of who the person used to be ... like their consciousness from pre-transition."

"How come I've never heard of it before?"

"They're not really that common and are really fucking hard to get a hold of, but since your aunt's a witch, she could've used a tracker spell to locate one."

My mind is on overload, nearly combusting with

thoughts of who was using the Transition Re-programmer and what they're transitioning into. It's almost too much to take in.

I struggle to keep my voice even. "But if that's what I heard, then that means either my aunt or Jayse is transitioning into something."

"I know." His voice is soft, careful.

Goddammit! Everything is so messed up. I just want things to go back to normal before I got my Guardian mark. My grandpa would be alive, and Jayse and I would still be close enough that he would just tell me what's going on.

I squeeze my eyes shut, crossing my fingers that I dreamed the last month and I'll wake up. But when I open my eyes, I'm still lying on my bed with the phone pressed to my ear and a giant void in my heart.

"How am I supposed to find out if someone's transitioning?" I ask more to myself. "And what they're transitioning into?"

"Have they done anything strange lately? Like change into a beast on a full moon? Drink blood? Sprout horns and scales?"

"No horns or scales, but honestly, I have no idea about the rest … I haven't spent that much time with either of them lately."

"You could always do a test."

"What kind of test?"

"Dump holy water on them. Touch them with iron. Pierce their skin with silver and see if it burns." The anger piercing his tone makes me wonder if someone did a test on him.

"That sounds like an awful thing to do to someone I care about," I say, sitting up on the bed.

"You'd be surprised how many people don't give a shit about hurting people they care about."

"Well, I'd rather not hurt my aunt or Jayse. Eventually, they'll tell me what's going on." I have to believe they will, because the truth is too hard to bear—that they'll never tell me because they don't trust me.

It takes him a moment to answer. "You're different from how I thought you were going be."

"How'd you think I was going to be? Coldhearted and mean?"

"Less compassionate and more like a Keeper."

I grimace as I think about Vivianne with her anti-Keeper attitude and how, when I return next week to the Academy, I get to spend detention with her.

"Not all Keepers are uncompassionate."

"But a lot of them are," he replies matter-of-factly.

"I've seen them kill things based solely on what they are instead of if they've committed crimes."

I want to argue, but there are Keepers who would torture someone they love if they thought they were transitioning into something inhuman. They might even consider killing them, consider their souls dead along with the person they once loved.

"Well, I'm not like that," I promise. "And neither is my family."

A beat or two skips by before he says, "I hope so for your aunt and cousin's sake. But, if I were you, I'd keep this little talk of ours to yourself, at least until you've figured out what's going on."

"Thanks. I will. And thanks for helping me. You just saved me a crap-load of time reading through a bunch of boring-ass books."

"Yeah, I've been there. Almost every new case requires a little bit of book research, some more than others. It's such a pain in the ass."

"I bet." I pause, debating whether or not to ask. Fuck it. Might as well try. "You wouldn't by chance want to save me a few more hours and tell me what electi means, would you? Otherwise, I'm going to have to hit the books again."

"You won't find that in a book ... And I thought I told

you to forget about that." He goes from hot to cold in two seconds flat. "I have to go, okay? I'm sorry. I'll see you next week when you get back."

He hangs up before I can get another word in.

I sigh, press end, and toss my phone aside.

"He knows what it is," I mutter as I climb off my bed. "I just need to figure out a way to get it out of him."

I wonder, though, why Jax told me about the Transition Re-programmer when he's being all hush-hush about electi. It has to be something terrible, like really, really, get-yourself-killed-over-talking-about-it terrible.

As I start to get ready for the funeral, putting on the nicest black dress I can find, I try to come up with a game plan for when I get back to the Academy, not only to pry information about electi out of Jax, but to steer clear of Vivianne as much as possible. But avoiding the Head of Interrogation and the woman who basically runs the Academy isn't going to be easy, especially when she thinks I'm hiding the dagger, which yeah, I technically am, but I'll never tell her that.

With a heavy sigh, I zip up the dress. Returning to Virginia in a few days makes me feel depressed, but at the same time, a tiny part of me wants to go. Do I hate leaving my family, hate that I'll be living clear across the country in a school run by a spiteful woman who hates my entire family? Heck yeah. But I'll also get to help solve my grandpa's murder, and right now, I want nothing more than to capture whoever took his life. Hopefully, I can help clear his name, because no matter what anyone says, I know my grandpa stole that dagger for a good reason.

I just hope I can figure out why before someone finds out I have it.

Chapter 17

All Foreseer funerals take place in the City of Crystal. The main form of transportation to the city is with a Foreseer, which basically means being sucked through a crystal ball. It's a strange sensation really, as if all your limbs are detached from your body while you tumble down a seemingly endless tunnel until finally landing in a massive, crystal cave that sparkles and shimmers from the domed ceiling to the glass floors.

Whenever my grandpa brought me here, I always had a smile on my face by the time I landed, mainly because the experience reminded me of riding a cracked-out merry-go-round. Today, though, I nearly burst into tears at the familiarity and memories. I keep my emotions under control, though, as I make my way with my mom and dad to the Glass Sea of Essence, which will soon be my grandpa's final resting place.

Hardly anyone has shown up for the funeral other than my family, Jayse's family, my grandma, and a few Foreseers. Even Elliot—a Foreseer around my age, whom my grandpa took under his wing and trained—isn't there.

Jayse refuses to make eye contact with me when we approach the sea, keeping his eyes trained on his feet. I consider going over and chatting with him to see if he'll slip up and give me a few clues on what's going on with him, but I decide now isn't really the right time.

"Where is everyone?" I ask my mom as I peer around the small crowd standing in a half circle around the quartz shoreline.

My mom's watering violet eyes are locked on the silvery liquid sea stretching before us. "Some felt that coming here ... that paying respects to him ... wouldn't be in their best interests, considering ..." She covers her mouth with her hand, choking back a sob.

I put my arm around her, trying to soothe her until my dad strides up and pulls her against him. He smoothes his hand up and down her back, saying, "It's going to be okay, honey. Just breathe, okay?"

"It's just so cruel," she whispers hoarsely. "He's not a bad man, and anyone who met him should know that."

"Deep down, everyone does," my dad tries to reassure her. "People just get caught up in the drama and gossip."

She rests her cheek against my dad's chest. "There's

no way he stole that dagger … I just wish I could prove it."

"We will," my dad vows to her.

"How are you holdin' up, hon?" My grandma appears by my side and offers me a sad smile.

"Shouldn't I be asking you that?" I ask, noting how exhausted she looks.

She traces her thumb under her bloodshot eyes before tucking a few strands of her long, grey hair behind her ear. "I'm fine." A fierceness flares in her eyes. "I have to be. Falling apart isn't an option."

"Grandma, no one's going to think less of you if you cry."

Her gaze glides to me. "Maybe you should be taking your own advice."

"I've cried." I turn to watch the sea ripple. "I just choose not to do it in front of anyone."

"What a coincidence. So do I." Her tone implies I'm full of shit.

I sigh. "I want to keep it together for my mom. She doesn't need to see me fall apart … She can barely keep it together already."

"You and I are so much alike it's scary sometimes." My grandma pulls me in for a hug, and being about six inches taller than her, I have to lean down a little in order to hug her back. "Maybe, after the funeral is over, we can sit down and have a good cry together."

"Sounds kind of weird," I say in a light tone, trying to keep myself as upbeat as I can, "so I'm down."

She chuckles with her gaze fastened on the sea. "Only you could make me laugh at a time like this."

I'm about to say I learned from the best when a hush falls across the crowd. Moments later, a line of Foreseers push through the gathering, wearing their ceremonial attire—a floor-length, silver cloak. Their leader guides them to the shoreline, his fingers wrapped around a glowing lavender orb, the shade strikingly similar to my grandpa's and my eyes.

I smash my lips together, knowing inside the orb is my grandpa's essence, his Foreseer power, and everything that made him the good, kind man he was. The orb will be placed into the water, and his power will essentially be set free to the sea with the rest of the deceased Foreseers.

No one utters a word as the leader crouches down and sets the ball into the water. Instead of sinking like expected, the orb floats, bobbing with the waves until the light inside flickers out.

Gone. Just like my grandpa.

I swear to God, I hear my grandpa whisper, *I'm not*

gone yet. But it could be the wind or my hope that some-how he's still nearby.

Please don't go.

A heart-wrenching sob echoes through the cave at the same time the crowd gasps. It takes me a second to process that the sob came from me.

Hot tears spill down my cheeks as I collapse to my knees.

My grandma sinks to the ground beside me, circling her arms around me. "It's going to be okay," she whispers through her tears. "It has to be. Everything will return to normal one day. It's what your grandpa would want."

I bob my head up and down, but only to comfort her. Deep down, I know our lives will never be what they once were. Too much has changed.

And it's only going to get worse, my grandpa's voice fills my head.

I tense in my grandma's arms, but she doesn't seem to notice as she continues to fall apart in my arms.

"It burnt out," she chokes. "The orb burnt out ... That's not supposed to happen ..."

I pull back and look at the silvery sea that has shifted to an eerie dark grey and then at the startled look on the face of the Foreseers' leader.

"If it's not supposed to burn out, then what's supposed to happen?" I ask.

"The light's supposed to join the sea ... so his essence is free ... But it burned out ..." Her shoulders tremble as she fights back the tears. "It burnt out."

A sense of dread weighs in the air. "I'm sorry, Grandma, but I still don't get why that's so bad."

She shakes her head several times while staring out at the sea. "Because it means your grandfather's essence wasn't in the orb. It means his essence is gone."

Shock numbs my body. "Gone where?"

But no matter what the answer, the situation is bad. An essence is like the spirit or soul of a person. Without it, a living person can become evil. When a person dies without an essence, they never truly get peace in the Afterlife.

"I have no idea ... I can't believe this ... I just don't understand," she mumbles to herself. "Did he lose it before or after he died? If it was before ..." Her voice lowers as she stares down at the fiery gold Keeper's mark on her arm. "Maybe that's why he did all those horrible things. Maybe he wasn't himself."

"Horrible *things*? As in plural? I thought he just took the dagger." Confusion swirls through my mind. "What else did he do?"

"Oh, Alana." Tears cascade down her cheeks. "Some of the stuff he got into right before he …" She sucks in a shaky breath. "And the people he was associating with … I love my husband and will do everything in my power to clear his name, but some of the stuff he was doing … Well, I'm going to have a long, hard road ahead of me to prove his innocence."

I start to ask her for more details, but she waves me off, pushing to her feet.

"I can see where your head is going, and this is neither the time nor place to talk about it." Her gaze darts to the crowd as her expression hardens. "So, they've decided to end it early? Figures."

I frown at the people leaving, whispering and gossiping about how they're not going to stick around to pay respects to a man who probably traded his essence for the dagger. Even one of my grandpa's closest friends joins in on the gossip, and I glare at him until he looks uncomfortable.

It might seem like my grandpa traded his essence for the dagger, but I know him better than that. He never would have given his essence up willingly.

No, someone or something had to have stolen it from him.

Entranced

My grandma suddenly grows rigid by my side. "What on earth is going on?"

I track her gaze to eight figures, all with similar sunken facial features and boney limbs. Worn, wispy fabric covers their bodies and floats behind them, moving like ribbons in the wind. I have no clue who or what they are, but everyone who was leaving has turned to gape at the skeleton-like people in horror.

"Who are they?" I whisper to my grandma.

She swallows hard. "Water Fey."

My jaw nearly cracks the glass floor below my feet. Water Fey? Shit. Water Fey are kind of like the law enforcement of our world, which can only mean one thing. Someone has committed a crime and is about to become a prisoner. But the real question is ...

"Since when can they come up on land? And how the heck did they get into the City of Crystal? Because I always thought they were limited to the lake in front of the Keepers' castle."

Usually, when someone commits a crime, a Keeper takes the prisoner and throws them into the lake to be dragged down to The Underworld by the Water Fey. They never come up on land.

"I have no idea." She shakes her head in disbelief as

she gapes at the Fey.

"Jocelyn Lucas," one of the male Water Fey says to my grandma as he stops in front of us. The rest of the Fey follow his lead and slow to a halt just behind him. "The queen has requested a word with you."

The Queen of the Underworld. No effing way is my grandma going with the Water Fey to talk to the queen. She's nothing but pure evil.

I position myself in front of my grandma and intervene. "Why? She didn't do anything."

The Water Fey glares at me like I'm the scum on the bottom of his boney foot. "And you are?"

"That's none of your damn business." My grandma steps in front of me, blocking me from the Fey's view. "You're here for me."

The Water Fey glowers at her. "I'm well aware of whom I'm here for."

My mother shoves her way through the crowd with rage blazing in her eyes. "And are you aware that the woman you're ordering to come with you is also a Keeper, and therefore, you have no jurisdiction over her?"

"I'm not here to sentence her," the Water Fey replies, scowling at my mom with annoyance. "I'm merely here to carry out a message that the queen has requested a word with her."

"You know there's no way a Keeper is going to willingly enter the queen's territory," my mom snaps, trembling with rage.

The Fey's hollow eyes cut to my grandma. "The queen will be willing to come on land if that is necessary."

"But the queen can die in the mortal world." My grandma eyes over the Water Fey suspiciously. "Why is she willing to risk her life simply to talk to me?"

"Her life is already at risk," he replies calmly. "Talking to you might be the only thing that can save her."

My grandma considers the request for a nerve-wracking amount of time. "Are Keepers allowed to be present with me?"

"If you wish not to be alone with the queen, then I can permit a few Keepers to accompany you," he responds curtly. "But we need to leave this moment. The queen's time on land is limited."

My grandma nods once then turns to my mother, who looks more than ready to remain at my grandma's side and go with her.

"I'd prefer it to not be you," she says to my mom with a hopeful look. "I can call someone else, tell them to meet me at the lake."

"I don't care what you prefer." My mom refuses to budge. "I'm not about to let the only parent I have left go without me to talk to the queen who has a reputation for her torture tactics."

My grandma sighs exhaustedly. "I know you're not, but I'd feel like a terrible mother if I didn't at least try to talk you out of going."

"I'm going with you, too." My father steps forward and places his hand on my mom's shoulder.

"What about me?" I ask. "Can I come?"

"No," the three of them say simultaneously.

Yeah, I knew that was coming, but I wouldn't be me if I didn't try.

"You can go home with your aunt and uncle," my mom says. "And wait with them until we get back." When I open my mouth to argue, she cuts me off. "I'm not arguing about this. I need to know you're safe while we're gone."

The worried, almost pained look on her face causes me to keep my mouth shut. I nod then watch my family leave with the Water Fey, wondering if they will be okay. Wondering what on earth the queen wants to talk to my grandma about. Wondering if they're in danger, and if I'll never see them again.

Chapter 18

After my grandma and parents leave the City of Crystal with the Water Fey, a Foreseer foresees me, my aunt, uncle, and a very quiet Jayse back home. Once we've all landed in the Hale's living room, the Foreseer leaves and the four of us settle in front of the fireplace with hot chocolate, cookies, and a very heavy amount of unsettling silence.

"I'm sure everything's okay," Aunt Aislin mumbles over the crackling fire.

I cup my untouched mug of hot chocolate in my hands. "How do you think the Water Fey managed to get on land? They're supposed to be strictly limited to the lake, right?"

"Maybe … not always." Uncle Laylen's brows pull together, as if he's confused himself as much as he just confused me.

"What does that mean?" I straighten in the chair and set the mug down on the coffee table. "Uncle Laylen, are you saying you know a way for them to come up on land?"

He mulls something over while chewing on his bottom lip. "If the queen were working with someone who could go back and change when the Water Fey were banished to the lake by the Keepers ..." He casts a worried glance at me before averting his gaze to the fire.

"You mean, if a Foreseer altered the vision, a Foreseer like my grandpa." I'm unsure whether to be mad at my Uncle Laylen for suggesting such a thing or worried that he could be right.

"I'm not saying it was necessarily your grandfather," he adds quickly. "It could be any Foreseer."

"Like Elliot," Jayse speaks for the first time since we arrived at his house.

"Why would Elliot free the Water Fey?" I ask. "He has no reason to."

"He's had no reason to do a lot of things he's done." His eyes are glued to the fire. "Like trying to tamper with visions."

Jayse and many Foreseers have distrust issues with Elliot. Yeah, he's done some questionable things, but he's never harmed anyone purposely. Besides, he's always been nice to me, so I usually defend him, but with him skipping out on my grandpa's funeral, I don't feel like making excuses for him. Still, I don't think it could be him.

"I doubt Elliot's powerful enough to alter a vision and keep it so we still remember the banishment happened," I say. "That's a complicated change that'd take a lot of power. And there'd have to be a reason to free the Water Fey from the lake to begin with." I rub my neck, trying to massage the kink out of it. "I think that reason has to do with my grandma."

Jayse's gaze swings to me, and for the briefest second, I swear his eyes glow red. It happens so quickly I can't be positive if I just imagined it.

"You think your grandma had something to do with freeing them?" he questions with a cock of his brow.

"I don't think she helped free them or anything like that. She was as surprised as everyone else when they showed up," I say. "But they were there for her, so she has to be connected to why they're free."

"Maybe whoever freed the Fey did it so they could talk to your grandma," Jayse suggests. "I mean, it's not like your grandma would ever go down to The Underworld to converse with the queen. Anyone knows that'd be a suicide mission. Even the queen knows it."

"But what could possibly be so important to tell my grandma that someone would risk freeing the Water Fey?" I reach for my mug. "Because, if they erased the moment they were banished, then they can now roam the world, which if I'm remembering correctly from my history lessons, means they'll use their torturing skills on humans."

Jayse gives a shrug. "Maybe we're wrong. Maybe a witch or something did a temporary spell, giving them visitation to land."

I take a sip of my hot chocolate. "Can a witch do that?"

My uncle Laylen, Jayse, and I all look to Aislin for an answer.

She appears taken aback, pressing her hand to her chest. "I haven't heard anything suggesting such a thing, but I also don't know a lot about black magic, and the kind of power it'd take to break a banishment would require a heavy amount of black magic."

"That means it might be possible, though." Maybe I'm being naïve, but I'm not ready to accept the Foreseer-changing-vision theory just yet. After all, if that theory ends up being true, then I know my grandfather will end up becoming a suspect.

"I don't know, Alana." She leans forward to grab a cookie off the plate on the table. "I think maybe we should stop worrying about this. I'm sure we will get some answers when your parents and grandma get back."

I check the time on the clock. It's been over three

hours since they left with the Water Fey, and with each tick of the clock, I grow more nervous. What if my worry is justified? What if they don't return?

"Would you relax, Alana?" Jayse's cold tone sends a chill up my spine. "It's making me nervous just watching how nervous you are."

I tear my attention from the clock and focus on him. He's staring at the flames again, his eyes dark against the glow, his mouth set in a firm line.

"I'm sorry." I take a deep breath, trying to chill out. But my nerves are too frazzled, and I can barely hold still. "It's just hard to relax when my family is with Water Fey and a queen known for her torture."

With his jaw clenched, he leaps to his feet. "I have to go. I'm supposed to be on a mission tonight." With that, he hurries out of the room, calling over his shoulder. "I'm so sorry, Alana. I really am. Please forgive me for everything."

It hurts to see him leave, but it also raises my suspicions that the Transition Re-programmer was for him. I remember what Jax said about testing the theory, and for a split, mind-losing second, I consider chasing Jayse down and poking him with iron, dousing him with salt, putting a cross to his skin. Then I come to my senses.

No matter what's going on with Jayse, he's still been my best friend for seventeen years. The last thing I ever want to do is hurt him.

"He's been working really hard lately," Aunt Aislin mutters as Jayse bails out the front door. "I think it's taking a lot out of him."

"But everything's okay with him, right? I mean he …" I'm not sure exactly what to say. "He seems really tired."

"He hasn't been sleeping very well." Uncle Laylen looks exhausted himself. Bags reside under his bloodshot eyes, and he keeps yawning every few minutes. "I'm so sorry, Alana."

I'm not sure why everyone keeps apologizing to me. It's not like Jayse has done anything to me other than be a bit distant.

"Would you guys quit apologizing? I'm okay. I swear."

Aislin picks at the corner of her cookie. "You're a good friend to Jayse. I know he's been distant lately … Please, just don't give up on him. He might not show it, but he needs you right now."

"I'm not planning on it." I watch the steam rise from my mug, swirling in the air like magic. "He's okay, though, right? Other than not getting enough sleep and working too hard ..." I raise my gaze to them. "There's nothing else going on?"

They trade an anxious look before Aislin sets the cookie down on the plate and turns to me.

"I really think you need to talk to him about it," she tells me. "It's not our place to tell you—tell anyone, for that matter."

My gaze flicks between the two of them. "But something's going on with him, isn't there?"

She nods. "There is ... It's why he's been acting so different lately."

"But he'll be okay?" God, I hope he's okay.

She hesitates, her eyes bubbling with tears. "I think, after he adjusts, he will."

Laylen reaches over and clasps her hand. "Honey, everything's going to be okay. We'll get through this."

"I hope so." She dabs her eyes with a handkerchief. "I'm just so worried about him."

"Maybe I should chase him down and talk to him," I suggest, already getting to my feet.

Knock. Knock. Knock.

"Hold that thought." Aislin leaps to her feet and rushes out of the room.

I sink back down in the sofa and take my phone out

from the pocket of my cardigan to text Jayse.

Me: Hey, I just wanted to make sure you're okay ... You ran out of here so quickly.

Jayse: I'm fine. I'm sorry I had to bail on you today. I know you really needed me. I just ... There's some stuff I have to take care of.

Me: You're okay, though, right? Your mom said you were going through some stuff.

Jayse: I am, but it's no excuse. I've been a really shitty friend the last couple of weeks.

Me: Is it because I'm not a Keeper? Is that why you haven't told me?

Jayse: No ... I haven't told you because I'm embarrassed.

Me: Jayse, you know I'd never judge you.

Jayse: I know, and I'll tell you, but not through text. It has to be in person. Can you meet me at the hideout in the morning?

Me: As long as everything goes okay with my parents and grandma.

Jayse: K. Text me when you know for sure. I have to go. Sorry.

Me: K. And you don't need to be sorry. We're good. I promise.

I put the phone away right as my dad and Aunt Aislin enter the living room. I jump to my feet, searching for injuries on my dad. Other than appearing a little bit worn out, he seems perfectly okay.

Thank God.

"Where's grandma and mom?" I wind around the coffee table, heading toward him.

"They're at home, resting," he says. "They're okay, just tired."

"What happened with the Water Fey and the queen?" I ask. "And did you figure out how they were able to come up on land?"

"Everything is such a mess. I don't even know where to start." He rakes his fingers through his hair, blowing out a stressed breath. "Alana, I never want you to think ill of your grandpa, but what I'm going to tell you ..." He takes a seat in an armchair, shaking his head. "Just remember we don't know everything yet. There may be a good reason for why he did what he did."

I numbly sit down on the edge of the coffee table. "He freed the Water Fey, didn't he?"

He offers me a remorseful look. "He traveled back to when they were banished and changed that moment from our history. Well, not so much changed as freed them by altering a vision later on. It's why we can still remember the banishment."

Aunt Aislin gasps as she sinks down on the sofa beside Uncle Laylen. "Oh, God ... I can't believe he'd do that ... It has to be a mistake."

I feel sick to my stomach. "Why would he do something like that?"

"We're not sure," my dad says, his gaze skimming the three of us. "The Fey and the queen were pretty vague about the details. But they did say that we'd find out in time. Whatever the hell that means."

"So are the Fey free now?" Uncle Laylen asks. "They can roam our world whenever they want?"

My dad nods as he slumps back in the chair. "They can, and they are, which means we need to prepare. The Keepers set up a meeting for tomorrow morning to come up with a plan. I hope you can make it."

Uncle Laylen props his foot on his knee and restlessly bounces his leg up and down. "Of course I'll make it. This is the Water Fey we're talking about. Those things are nothing but trouble. We need to get them banished back to the lake."

"I know we do," my dad agrees. "God, I still can't believe what the queen said to Jocelyn, and then she had the audacity to try and convince us that everything would be okay."

"Wait. Why did the queen want to talk to grandma? I'm guessing it wasn't just to tell her about what grandpa did." My stomach churns at the thought of my grandpa releasing the Fey.

There has to be a good reason, I try to tell myself. *He would never do it without a good reason.*

"Apparently, your grandpa made a deal with the queen." Disappointment crosses my dad's face. "And the queen made a promise to him to pass along a message to Jocelyn that she's not supposed to go looking for your grandpa's essence."

"But why would Julian free the Fey just so the queen could pass along that message?" Aislin wonders, clasping the moon pendant of her necklace. "That doesn't make any sense."

"That wasn't the only reason he freed them," my dad explains. "The queen made sure we understood that, but she wouldn't explain why. She kept saying 'all in good time' until we grew so frustrated we left."

"Can she remain on land now?" I ask. "The queen, I mean."

My dad swiftly shakes his head. "She had to return to

The Underworld; otherwise, her kingdom will collapse. But she can still occasionally visit, so we need to find a way to banish her and her Fey to The Underworld again."

"Why not just do it like you did last time?" I suggest. "That seems like the easiest way, doesn't it?"

"It's not that simple. There's a lot in the history books about the banishment, but no specific details about how the seal was created in the first place." My dad reaches forward and pats my knee. "I don't want you to worry about this. This is the Keepers' problem."

"I want to help," I say. "Please let me help with this, Dad."

"You can help by going to the Academy and following through with your training," he tells me. When I start to protest, he lifts his hand, silencing me. "You'll be safe there. And that's what everyone needs right now—for you to be safe and away from all the rumors about your grandpa. I want you to stay as far away from this mess as possible and remember your grandpa for the man he was, not the man everyone's going to accuse him of being."

I nod, even though I have no plans of staying out of this. Yeah, I'll go back to the Academy, but now I'm even more motivated to solve my grandpa's death and find out who stole his essence. My parents just don't need to know that; otherwise they'll try to stop me.

The queen might have warned my grandma not to look for it, but that doesn't mean I'm not going to.

Chapter 19

I spend the rest of the night getting ready to return to the Academy tomorrow. I wasn't supposed to go back for a few more days, but my dad made arrangements for me to return early, wanting me out of the way as soon as possible.

I decide not to take the dagger back with me. It'll be safer here. So while everyone's in the kitchen, chatting about what happened at my grandpa's funeral, I steal a handful of fairy ash from my mom's stash to bury with the dagger, because it should help conceal the location. Then I sneak outside to Jayse's and my hideout—a small cave in the side of a dirt hill located in the middle of the forest.

The place is ideal for hiding out or hiding something. Hardly anyone knows it's there besides my family and Jayse's, and Aunt Aislin put a bunch of enchantment spells on it. The spells make it impossible for anyone other than the Hale's and Lucas's to see the cave. It's supposed to be for safety reasons, but Jayse and I ended up turning it into a place for us to hide out.

Entranced

With the flashlight in my hand, I make my way through the forest. Fortunately, I'm not afraid of the dark since the moon and stars offer little light. I keep my phone clutched in my free hand in case I need to call my parents, but honestly, I find the quiet of the forest comforting, or at least, I used to. With all that's been happening—deaths, warnings from my grandfather, the Water Fey being free— I'll admit I'm feeling a little skittish. Every snap of a tree branch and noise of an animal makes the hairs on the back of my neck stand on end.

I quicken the pace, speed walking to the hill. Once I'm safely inside the cave, I balance the flashlight in the center, grab a small shovel, and quickly dig a hole beneath a chest. I try to ignore the memories creeping up on me, but Jayse and I used to spend so much time in here I can't help missing those days.

"Everything seemed so simple back then." I sigh, drop the dagger into the hole along with the fairy ash, bury both with the dirt, and drag the chest back over it. "That should keep it safe for a while," I say as I dust my hands off.

Then I head for the ladder and climb back up. Once I crawl out of the hillside, I slide down the dirt to the bottom. Brushing the dirt off my ass, I start back through the forest with the flashlight aimed in front of me.

I make it quite a ways without running into any problems, but branches seem to be snapping all around me, and then a wolf howls from somewhere.

A chill slithers up my spine as I glance up at the moon. "It's not full. You're okay."

As if wanting to prove me wrong, I spot a white figure from my peripheral vision. I swing around and jump back, my heart racing in my chest as I aim the flashlight at it. The figure moves at an inhuman speed, dodging behind a tree. I should run, but the eyes of the figure make me pause.

They're violet.

"Grandpa?" I cautiously inch toward the tree he hid behind. "Grandpa, is that you?"

Another break of a branch. Another howl. Then the figure barrels toward me and knocks me flat on my back. The flashlight flies from my hands. Darkness smothers me.

Panicking, I flip over to my stomach and push to my feet. With my arms to my side, I squint through the darkness, breathing so loudly it makes me cringe.

"Grandpa, if that's you ... Please say something."

The only response I get is the eerie silence that has suddenly taken over the forest.

Reaching into my pocket, I whip out my phone and click on the flashlight app. It's not as bright as the flashlight itself, but it works.

I shine the light around the pine trees and overgrown bushes, but I can't find a sign of the figure anywhere. I'm not ready to give up just yet, though.

I stay out there for at least an hour, looking around before I give up.

"Maybe it was just your imagination," I say to myself.

But I know I saw something: either my grandpa, his ghost, or someone who looked an awful lot like him.

Chapter 20

I check on the cave before I leave. When I'm satisfied the dagger is still safe, I hike back home and slip into my room to finish packing.

Jayse texts me while I'm folding up my clothes and stuffing them into my suitcase.

Jayse: Hey, I'm sorry to do this, but I can't meet you in the morning. I have some stuff to do, and then I have the Keeper's meeting.

Me: How about tonight? I can wait up.

Jayse: Sorry, I'm out right now.

I sigh in frustration.

Me: Are you sure you're not just procrastinating this? Sometimes you do that.

Jayse: I swear I'm not. And to prove it, I'm going to make a trip out to Virginia so we can hang out for a few days and talk.

Me: When?

Jayse: Soon. I promise.

Me: Okay. If you need to talk about anything at all, I'm here for you.

Jayse: I know. You're a good friend. I wish I could be a better one to you.

Me: You are a good friend. You always have been.

Jayse: I hope you think so after I tell you.

I'm about to text him back that of course I will when another message buzzes through.

Jayse: I have to go. I'll text you when I know I'm coming out there.

Me: All right. TTYL

I put the phone away and concentrate on finishing packing.

Poor Jayse. Whatever's going on with him has got him worried I'll somehow judge him. I'd never do that to him. But I have to wonder if any of the Keepers know yet. I doubt it, or else he wouldn't be out on a mission. In fact, they might banish him from the group or, worse, harm him.

"I'm so sorry you can't stay longer." My grandma enters the room as I'm zipping up my suitcase. "But I think this is for the best. I know your grandpa wouldn't want you involved in this mess."

"That's what everyone keeps saying." I prop the bag against the foot of the bed. "Grandma, when you said grandpa was associating with bad people before he died, who were they?"

"Oh, honey, I don't want you to worry about that." She smoothes my hair out of my eyes, something she did when I was a child. "I don't want your grandpa's problems to become your burden."

"I'm helping with his case," I tell her. "And anything you could tell me will be helpful."

Her mouth plummets to a frown. "Are you sure you want to do that? It might be best to let someone else handle it."

I shake my head. "I have to do this. It's important."

Her arm falls to her side as she sighs. "I guess I kind of understand, but promise me you'll be careful. The people he was associating with … I think they were dangerous."

I flop down on the edge of my bed and stretch out my legs. "So you know who they are?"

She takes a seat beside me and stares at the backs of her hands. "I only met them once, and they never gave out names. They looked human, but they had the strangest mark on them, like a serpent shaped in a backward three."

"I've never seen a mark like that before," I say. "But I bet there's something in the Keepers' records."

"I already checked and couldn't find anything. I did

accidentally overhear a phone conversation between these people and your grandfather. I'm not sure what exactly it was about, but I did hear him mention something about a war."

My heart slams against my chest. "I heard grandpa mention a war, too. Quite a few times in my dreams."

Her attention whips to me. "He was dreamwalking?"

"I'm not positive, but I think so. I mean … It felt like it was really happening." I consider telling her that I thought I saw him in the forest, but then I'd have to explain what I was doing out there.

"I don't know what to say. Dreamwalking's forbidden. If the Foreseers found out …" Her shoulders sag as she sighs. "Well, I guess it doesn't really matter. He's already in enough trouble as it is." She twists to face me. "How many times has he done it?"

"A couple of times before he died and once after." I scratch my head. "He keeps warning me about a war and of something called the electi."

A pucker forms at her brow. "Yeah, your mother asked me about that. I wish I knew who they are."

"I'm not sure if it's a who or a what. He never said. He only told me that I was in danger and then threw the word out there." I rest back on my elbows. "I've been researching the crap out of the word, but haven't found anything. I'm pretty sure Jax—my kinda, sorta mentor at the Academy—knows what it is, but he won't tell me. I'm going to find a way to pry it out of him. I just need to find his weak spot."

"Hmm … I might know a way to get it out …" Without finishing the sentence, she stands up and dashes out of the room.

Puzzled, I get up and follow her to the guestroom where she's been staying for the last week. By the time I walk in, she's rummaging around in the top drawer of the dresser.

"Your parents would kill me if they knew I'm giving you this." She tosses a few shirts and pairs of pants on the floor then removes a ring-sized box from the drawer. "But considering you might be in danger"—she faces me with the boxed clutched in her hand—"I really think you should know what you're up against." She sticks her hand out, urging me to take the box.

"What is it?" I pluck the box from her hand and lift the lid. "A ring?" I reach to remove it, but she swats my hand away.

She taps the silver band of the ring. "Make sure to only touch the silver part until you put it on. Once you touch the ruby, you'll end up confessing your secrets to anyone who will listen."

"Wait." I blink at her in shock. "Is this laced with truth serum?"

She nods. "All it should take is brushing the ruby across Jax's skin, and you should be able to get the truth out of him."

My stomach pangs with a hint of guilt. "It kind of feels wrong to manipulate him like that."

"I think, as long as you only get what you need out of him, you won't be in the wrong." When I'm still not fully convinced, she presses, "Alana, I've never been one for taking someone's freewill away from them, but until we find out what is going on, we'll never be able to clear your grandpa's name and find his essence. Plus, if he thinks you're in danger, we need to find out as much about this electi as we can."

I get where she's coming from, but I still feel a little guilty using the ring. "So, you're still going to look for his essence even after the queen warned you not to?"

"Of course. Your grandpa was the love of my life, and I fully plan on our essences reuniting one day, but that can't happen if his hasn't been properly laid to rest."

I snap the box lid shut. "Okay, I'll do it."

I don't realize how much she wants me to do it until relief washes over her face.

"You'll let me know what you find out?" she asks.

"I'll call you the second I do." I stuff the box into the back pocket of my striped pajama bottoms. "How'd you get this ring, though? Isn't truth serum, like, really, really rare?"

"I found it the other day, tucked away with some of your grandpa's old crystal balls. I'm not sure how long he's had it or where he got it from, but I thought I should hang on to it, just in case." She muses over something. "It's strange I found a use for it already. It's almost like he knew we were going to need it."

I nod, completely agreeing with her. Very strange, indeed.

It's almost as if my grandpa is still hanging around somehow, watching us.

Chapter 21

By the time I crawl into bed, I'm so exhausted I nearly pass out before my head even hits the pillow. I secretly hope to drift into a dream where I can talk to my grandpa, but I end up tumbling into a nightmare about Water Fey tying me up and peeling my skin from my body. It's a morbid dream for sure, but I can easily picture the Water Fey doing something like that. I learned enough in history class to know just how sick and twisted they are.

I wake up dripping in sweat and end up lying in bed, wide-awake, until the sun rises above the hills and paints the sky with an array of pinks and oranges. Since I have an early flight to catch, I drag myself out of bed, tug on a pair of jeans and a T-shirt, pull my hair into a ponytail, and head downstairs with my suitcase.

My parents are in the kitchen, drinking coffee and discussing the latest paranormal experimental facility they've discovered. I pause in the doorway, listening to them.

"I know we've got a lot going on," my mom tells my

dad as she adds a spoonful of sugar to her coffee, "but we still need to make time to look into this facility. And if necessary, we need to make a plan of action and destroy it."

My dad takes a drink from the coffee mug. "There's been so many lately. It can't be a coincidence. They have to be connected somehow."

With the funeral, this thing with Jayse, and the drama with the Water Fey, I almost forgot about the tagged zombie Jax showed me right before I left. It seems like such a long time ago, yet it was only last week. I wonder if I'll learn more about it when I return.

I blink at my reaction, startled at how comfortable I've gotten with the idea of being a Guardian.

"Hey, honey," my mom greets me with a weary smile. "Do you have everything packed?"

"Yeah." I open the fridge to grab a bottle of juice. "So, you guys found another paranormal experimental facility, huh?"

My dad reclines back in his chair. "Not just one. Three. They've been on the rise."

"Before I left the Academy, Jax showed me a tagged zombie." I twist the lid off the bottle of juice. "He said there's been a lot of dead ones coming in. Not just zombies, either. I wonder why there's so many."

Entranced

My dad gives a discreet glance at my mom. "We have a few theories."

I gulp down a swallow of juice before asking, "Which are ...?"

"That they're all run by the same person," my mom says. "We're just not sure who that person is."

"Why would someone want to experiment on things like zombies, though?" I ask. "It doesn't make any sense."

"That's what we're trying to find out." My dad rises from his chair, sets his empty mug in the sink, and then glances at my suitcases in the doorway. "Are you about ready?"

I nod. "Yeah. What time are we hitting the road?"

My dad glances at his watch. "We should probably get going. It's a little early, but we have to be back in time for the meeting."

My mother agrees with a nod then collects her purse and the car keys.

I say good-bye to my grandma before getting into the car, promising I'll call her as soon as I use the ring. My parents and I then drive in silence, and it reminds me of the last time we drove to the airport. But the quietness is broken when my dad slows the car to a stop at the back of a long line of vehicles. Considering we live way, way out in the middle of nowhere, the traffic is completely out of place.

"What the hell's going on?" he asks as he shoves the shifter in park.

My mom rolls down her window and pokes her head out to get a better look. "It looks like the road's blocked off."

My dad checks the time on the dashboard. "She's going to miss her flight ... and we're going to be late for the meeting."

"Just go around." She waves her hand for my dad to get a move on. "The traffic's not moving the other way, either."

He arches a brow at her. "Who are you and what have you done with my wife?"

I giggle for what feels like the first time in ages. "Yeah, Mom, since when did you become such a rule breaker?"

"I break the rules sometimes," she argues, offended.

My dad shoots me an *okay* look in the rearview mirror, and I muffle my laughter with my hand. My mom playfully swats his arm with a smile on her face. I smile, too, glad to see her happy again.

"I think Mom's right, Dad. Let's ditch this line and

swing around them."

He chuckles. "Fine, but if I get pulled over, I'm telling the officer it's not my fault, that my rule breaking wife made me do it." Waggling his brows at my mom, he shifts the car into drive and steers the car into the other lane.

A barricade blocks both sides of the road. As we near it, my dad cranes the wheel and heads for the grass area. Right before the wheels reach the grass, he taps on the brakes.

"Shit. It's the Guardians." He parks the car on the side of the road, the wheels kicking up a cloud of dust.

I scoot forward in the seat and take in the group of people on the other side of the barricade. They are all wearing black cargo pants and black T-shirts, and they're carrying clipboards as they walk around something on the ground.

"What is that?" I ask. "A dead body?"

My dad pushes the door open to get out. "You two stay here. I'm going to go see what's going on."

"No way." I climb out with him, ignoring the dirty look he gives me. "This is part of my life now. I'm going with you."

He shakes his head but doesn't argue. "You're right, but stay by my side just in case."

"Just in case what?" I joke as we hike through the grass toward the scene. "The dead body comes back to life?"

He gives me a tolerant look, but then a grin spreads across his face. "I'm glad to see your sarcasm is back. I've missed it."

I feel the slightest bit guilty for smiling so soon after my grandpa died, but at the same time … "It feels good to have it back."

Our smiles promptly fade when we arrive at the barricade, though. On the other side, splattered across the asphalt, is what looks like red paint. But the salty scent of rust haunts the air.

Blood.

And not just a little bit of blood; a whole freakin' ton covers the ground, the nearby trees and bushes, and the grass.

As we weave around the barricade, the stench becomes so overpowering I nearly dry heave.

"Wait here," my dad says before we reach the dead body. "I'm going to see what's going on." He strides off toward a taller man carrying a clipboard who seems to be ordering everyone around.

"It looks like something was massacred." I cover my

hand over my nose and mouth to block out the stench.

"That's because something was."

The sound of Jax's voice elicits a shiver from me, the good kind of shiver that makes my stomach go all kinds of crazy.

Seriously. What the hell is wrong with me? This a totally inappropriate time to get all hot and bothered.

I summon a deep breath before turning around, ordering myself not to check him out. But I can't help sneaking a peek.

The corner of his lip tugs up into a cocky, half grin. "It's kind of inappropriate to be checking me out right now."

"I wasn't checking you out." Mental happy dance! My voice came out even! "I was looking at the blood on your shirt."

"Sure you were," he says condescendingly. "And it's not blood. It's ketchup from the hamburger I just ate."

I scrunch up my nose. "You ate at a crime scene, with that"—I swing my arm in the direction of the dead body—"right there?"

He lifts a shoulder, shrugging. "I was hungry, and I'm not leaving anytime soon."

"It's still gross."

"You get used to it."

"I doubt it." I cast a glance at the dead body covered by a sheet then look back at Jax. "You could've told me you were out here working a case thirty miles from my home."

"I just got here about an hour ago. I didn't really have much time to think about it."

I hug my arms around myself as a light breeze kicks up "How long ago was it killed?"

He nods his head, indicating for me to follow as he walks toward the body. "We received the call only a few hours ago."

I pay extra attention to the ground to make sure I don't step in any blood. "You guys didn't fly here?"

"Nah, we usually don't fly to cases." He draws his sunglasses over his eyes as the sunlight filters through the clouds. "Only when we're picking up new recruits."

"So how'd you get here, then?"

"By teleportation."

"You know a witch?" I don't know why I'm so surprised, considering the Academy is full of all sorts of otherworldly creatures.

He crouches down beside the covered up body. "We have a few of them who work for us. They help us with stuff, but you'll soon find that out once you start working more cases."

I stand a ways away from the body, the stench barely bearable. "Why not just use teleportation all the time, then? Because it seems a hell of a lot easier."

"Yeah, but it's never a good thing to rely on one thing so much, and flying's good for newbies. It's simple, un-complicated. Plus, Vivianne hates using magic unless it's completely necessary, like today when we needed to get here fast. If we didn't have to travel so quickly to murder scenes, we'd probably just fly all the time." He lifts the body, releasing the stench of rotting flesh.

I bite back the vomit burning at the back of my throat and force myself to really look. "What was it?"

He leans closer to examine the faceless skull. "We think it's another zombie."

"Another one? Do that many of them get murdered?"

"Not usually, but over the last couple of months, yes."

"But they're already dead. It doesn't make any sense."

He reaches into his pants pocket and retrieves a pair of latex gloves. "It might not make sense, but we're here to try and make some sort of sense out of it." He wiggles his fin-gers into the gloves. "And I have a theory." He raises his hand and motions for me to come closer.

189

"No thanks." I step back. "I'm cool up here, breathing zombie-dead-body-free air."

He shoots me an impatient look over his shoulder. "Would you please quit being a pain in the ass? I'm trying to teach you how to do our job."

I grind my teeth at the pain-in-the-ass remark but decide to let it go. "Fine." Begrudgingly, I inch forward and crouch down beside him.

His lips twitch as he struggles not to grin. "Now, was that so hard?"

"Yeah, it really was."

He frowns. "Do you enjoy being a pain in the ass?"

I smile sweetly at him. "About as much as you enjoy being a cocky asshole."

He shakes his head, but I detect a trace of a grin. "I've been looking for a tag on the zombie. I haven't found one yet, but I'm guessing there has to be one somewhere."

I shift my weight. "You think its death was related to the other zombie you showed me?"

He nods, squinting at the fleshless left cheek of the zombie. "I do. And I think their murders are both related to the same experimental facility."

"My parents think the same person runs all the experimental facilities."

His gaze snaps to me. "They told you that?"

I shake my head. "I overheard them talking this morning. I did talk to them about it for a little while."

"I'm surprised they'll talk to you about stuff like that. It's usually a pain in the ass to get information from Keepers."

"Yeah, but they're my parents. They're not going to treat me like shit because I'm a Guardian now."

"Then you're lucky ... to have such good parents." He sounds sincere, and it throws me off.

"Um, thanks."

He nonchalantly shrugs. Then, cocking his head to the side, he lifts up the zombie's arm and rotates it over. "I know there has to be a tag somewhere."

"Have you checked its legs?"

"I've checked everywhere."

"Hmmm ..." I push to my feet and walk around the body, scanning it over, looking for something Jax might have missed.

I peer under the sheet at his feet and legs. I have no clue why I'm being so ballsy all of a sudden or where the instinct is coming from, but Jax seems to find me entertaining as he watches me with amusement dancing in his eyes.

"Find anything?" he asks as I return to his side.

"No, but I might have a theory."

"Really?"

I nod, tucking a strand of my hair behind my ear. "Its face was scraped off, right?"

Jax keeps his eyes trained on me curiously. "We think it was pushed out in front of a moving vehicle that was going pretty fast, and the pavement ripped it off."

I shudder at the thought. "Well, what if the tag was on the face? I mean … the other zombie you showed me had it on its cheek."

He momentarily contemplates my idea before his lips pull up into a grin. "That's a pretty good, very accurate theory."

I narrow my eyes at him. "You already thought of that, didn't you?"

"Of course I did."

"Then why didn't you say so?"

"Because I wanted to see if you could come up with it on your own," he says simply. "You did it faster than I expected. You might end up being good at this after all."

I cross my arms and stare him down. "So, you thought I was going to suck?"

"At first I did," he says with a shrug. "But now"—another shrug—"I don't know. You might not suck as badly as I thought."

Okay, I so don't feel guilty that I'm going to use that ring on him anymore.

"Gee, thanks." My voice drips with sarcasm. "It's always great to be told you won't suck as badly as someone thought."

His lips quirk. "You're welcome."

We trade a defiant look, but I'll admit I'm finding our bickering more amusing than annoying.

"So, what else do you know about its murder?" I peer around at the other Guardian's inspecting the crime scene.

He cocks his brow. "Is that curiosity I detect in your tone?"

"I don't know." I play it cool. "Maybe."

His grin slips through as he straightens his legs to stand. "Come on. I'll show you what we've found so far."

"Alana, we need to get going," my dad says, hurrying toward us. "I talked to the person in charge, and they're going to let us go around on the side road over there." He points to the right at the trees. "There's one just a ways in there."

"Can we go in a few minutes?" I ask. "Jax was about to show me some stuff."

My dad glances at Jax in surprise, as if just noticing

him. "Jax, it's good to see you again."

Jax tugs off his gloves and shakes my dad's hand. "You, too, sir."

I roll my eyes. I'm so going to give him shit for the sir remark.

"Are you working this case?" my dad asks.

He shakes his head. "I'm just helping out. I haven't officially been assigned to it yet, but I'm hoping."

My dad's gaze drops to the zombie on the ground. "There've been a lot of them showing up dead, hasn't there?"

Jax nods. "I think we've found a total of six within the last two months or so."

My dad bobs his head up and down, thinking about something. "Have you found any links between the deaths?"

Jax shifts his weight, scratching at the back of his neck. "I can't really give out that kind of information yet."

"I understand." My dad stares at the zombie for a second longer before looking back at me. "We really need to get going. Your flight leaves in an hour and a half."

I don't know why I'm so disappointed. I should be thrilled I don't have to hang out by a rotting dead body all day. Yet, somehow I'm not.

"If you don't care, sir, she can stay," Jax offers, as if sensing my unwillingness to go. "It might be good for her to get the experience since she missed the first week of classes."

My dad considers Jax's offer with his lips pressed in a thin line. "What about her flight?"

"She can teleport with me." Jax's gaze glides to me with amusement twinkling in his silver eyes. "Although, I know she'll be disappointed about not getting to fly again. She loved it so much the first time around."

I cross my arms and elevate my brows. "I did until you drugged me."

My dad's jaw drops as he sputters, "D-drugged you?"

"I didn't drug her," Jax says in a panic. "I just gave her some Otium to calm her."

My dad still looks pissed off, so I smooth the situation over before he decides to make me go to the airport.

"I was just kidding about the drug part, Dad," I say lightly. "I was freakin' out, and he gave me some Otium to calm me down."

My dad relaxes a smidgeon. "Well, as long as you knew you were taking it."

"I did," I assure him.

My dad nods, but tension lingers in his expression.

Still, he agrees to let me return to the Academy with Jax.

After I collect my bag from the trunk, I say good-bye to Mom and Dad.

"And, Alana," my dad says as he hugs me, "could you keep this whole Water Fey thing a secret for now? The Keepers don't want it getting out to anyone just yet."

"But don't the Foreseers know?" I ask. "They saw them at the funeral."

"They've made an agreement to keep silent until we can figure out more about what's going on," he explains, stepping back. "We want to try to avoid creating a panic. And the more people who know, the more we risk setting off a world-wide panic."

"All right, I won't tell anyone," I agree as I scoop up my bag from the ground.

He waves at me before climbing into the car with my mom. She cries as they pull away from the crime scene, and I almost tear up, too.

"You did better that time." Jax steps up beside me.

I tear my attention from the road and look at him. "Better with what?"

He stuffs his hands into his pockets. "Saying good-bye."

I let out a deafening exhale. "I thought it'd be harder

because of my grandpa, but I guess it was a little bit easier."

He checks his phone when it vibrates. "Maybe it's because you're getting used to the idea of being a Guardian."

"Maybe, or maybe I'm just getting more used to saying good-bye."

He gives me a sympathetic look before we start walking back toward the zombie, the gravel crunching under our shoes.

"Speaking of your grandpa," Jax says abruptly as he stuffs his phone into the back pocket of his cargo shorts, "I thought you'd like to know we already have a list of suspects."

"Really?" I perk up. "That's great news. Who are they?"

He hesitates. "I'm not sure if I can tell you just yet."

I put a hand on my hip. "Why not? You told me I could help, remember?"

"Yeah, but I'm worried you'll react irrationally and try to go all Keeper on them and off them one by one."

"Hey." I press my hand to my chest, offended. "I've never killed anyone before."

He gives me an accusing look. "But I know you've thought about it."

Okay, he has me there.

"If I promise not to assassinate them, will you tell me?" I just hope I can keep my promise because tracking down my grandpa's killer and offing them does sound sort of appealing.

Jax slows to a stop, folds his arms across his lean chest, and looks around at the road and trees surrounding us. "I'll tell you what. If you can find a clue that will help this case, then I'll show you the list."

Sounds easy enough.

I stick out my hand to shake on it. "Game on, werewolf dude."

Chapter 22

Okay, I was a little overzealous about being able to easily find a clue. Not only do I have to be careful everywhere I walk, but I'm not allowed to touch anything, which makes finding anything seemingly impossible.

After being scrutinized by multiple Guardians, I decide to venture into the forest to search for clues and to take a breather from the intensity of the situation. I hike a ways in before leaning against a thick tree trunk to rest and gather my thoughts.

I want to see that list really badly, but I'm not very confident I'll be able to find a clue. Sure, my dad and I used to watch a lot of mystery shows and movies when I was younger, but I don't think Scooby Doo-ing this is going to work.

"This is impossible." I huff out an exasperated breath. "I have no idea what I'm doing. Seriously, I'm starting to gain mad respect for Guardians."

"You want some help?"

Jax's voice startles the living bejesus out of me.

I gasp, pressing my hand to my chest. "Whoa, dude. A little warning before you go creeping up on someone in the woods."

He's resting against a tree trunk a few feet from me, looking as comfortable as can be. I wonder how long he's been standing there. I wonder if he just heard what I said.

"If you help me, then I don't win our bet, do I?" I square my shoulders and carefully take a step forward, searching the grass for anything out of the ordinary. "You can leave now. I've got this."

"You're a Guardian, too, Alana." Jax moves up behind me, and his werewolf scents—cologne, soap, and something woodsy—grace my nostrils. I try not to breathe them in, but I totally do. "You need to stop referring to yourself as being separate from our group."

I pick up a long, thin stick and use it to move tall blades of grass aside. "It kind of feels like I'm separate right now. I have no clue what I'm doing, unlike everyone else."

"Everyone else has been doing this for a while. You're new at it, but you'll get better."

"Everyone is acting like I'm in the way."

"That's because newbies usually don't get to work

such a big case." He continues to invade my personal space, matching every step I take.

I glance over my shoulder at him. "So ... Then why am I allowed to work on this case?"

He gives a half shrug. "Because I told them you were going to."

I turn around to face him then step back when I realize how close we are. He's so close I can feel his body heat and intensity pouring off him.

"Are you that high up that you can do that? I thought you said you weren't an investigator yet."

"I'm not as high up as I want to be, but yeah, I'm doing okay for now."

"But you're so young."

"Really?" His voice carries mocking sarcasm.

I roll my eyes. "You know what I mean. You seem really young to be successful already."

"I'm not that successful, and I have connections, which helps," he says. "Guardian blood runs in my family, and a lot of people respect us."

"Yeah, that's how everyone used to be with my family." I sigh and start poking the stick around in the grass again. "But ever since this whole stealing-the-dagger thing with my grandpa ... Well, a lot of Keepers and Foreseers have turned their backs on us."

"Yeah, people suck like that. Always jumping to con-clusions without the facts," he says, surprising me. "But at least you know who your true friends are, right?"

"I guess so. It still sucks, though. I know my grandpa. If he did steal the dagger like everyone is saying, then it was for a good reason."

"I know," he agrees.

I go all bug-eyed. "Wait, you don't think he's guilty?"

He shakes his head. "I've been working on his case, remember? I've researched him enough to know he was a good man. Yeah, he did a couple of iffy things, but I'm guessing the more I dig into it, the more I'll be able to dis-count a lot of the accusations."

I want to freakin' hug him, but deciding not to look like a total emotional psychopath, I refrain.

"I'm glad. He needs someone on his side." When tears prickle at my eyes, I turn around and busy myself with searching around a few trees.

He gives me a moment to collect myself before follow-ing me. "You know, you're on the right path," he says. "There is something out here. I can smell it."

I twist to face him, my curiosity piquing. "What do you mean you can smell it?"

He sniffs the air. "There's blood out here."

I take a whiff of the air. "All I smell are evergreens. "

"That's because you don't have werewolf senses." Smirking, he softly grazes his finger down my nose before swinging around me.

I shiver from his touch once again and come to the conclusion that my body may be more attracted to Jax than my mind. At least, that's what I try to convince myself.

"Where are you going?" I jog after him as he hikes deeper into the woods.

"Finding out where the blood is." He strides through the grass, moving around trees and bushes until finally slamming to a halt beside a large rock. "I think it's coming from up there."

"This is so unfair," I half gripe, half joke. "I could've found it first if I had a superhuman sense of smell."

He throws me another arrogant grin before running forward and lunging onto the top of the rock.

"Okay, now you're just showing off," I mutter with a shake of my head.

He must hear me because his grin expands.

I smirk back at him before approaching the rock. Then I grip the side and easily scale up to the top.

I dust off my hands, smiling proudly as he gapes at me.

"What? I live with a bunch of Keepers. I stay in shape, okay?"

He shakes his head, grinning, and then walks toward the center of the rock and bends down to pick something up.

I head toward him. "What is it?"

With his brows knit, he holds up a miniature, crystal ball filled with pieces of shimmering rubies. "It's a Foreseer Traveling Crystal, isn't it?" he asks.

Reality crashes against my chest. "It's my grandpa's."

Puzzlement etches into Jax's expression. "How could you possibly know that? I thought every Foreseer had one these?"

I swallow the lump in my throat as I reach forward and brush my fingertip along a deep chip on the crystal. "I was with him when he dropped it. We were on the roof of his house, watching a lunar eclipse, and it rolled off and cracked against the concrete. I told him he should just fix it, but he said he wanted to leave it there so he could always remember watching the eclipse with me."

It grows quiet as I stare at the crystal ball in disbelief. Why the hell would it be out here, nearby where a murder just took place?

I snap myself out of my trance. "Jax, we can't turn that

in for evidence. My grandpa's already in enough trouble as it is, and I'm sure Vivianne will make a big deal of it. She thinks he's guilty more than anyone."

"Alana, do you know how much trouble we could get in for tampering with evidence?" Jax shakes his head. "We have to turn it in. Besides, your grandpa couldn't have done this. The murder just happened only hours ago."

Yeah, but I'm pretty sure I just saw him last night in the forest by my house.

I'm not about to tell him that, though.

"Can we just hold onto it for a couple of days while I look into it?" I ask. When he doesn't cave right away, I clasp my hands together. "Please, Jax. At least give me a chance to find out why it was out here."

He warily glances from the crystal ball to me. "I'll give you a week."

Holy shit! I can't believe he agreed!

"Thank you. Thank you. Thank you!" I throw my arms around him, deciding to momentarily risk looking like an emotional psychopath.

He stiffens and awkwardly pats me on the back. "You're welcome, but if we get caught, it's all on you."

"I'll completely take the blame for it." I move back, lowering my arms to my sides. "If anyone finds out, I'll tell them I forced you to go along with my wicked plan."

"Let's not go overboard," he says, his lips twitching in-to a smile. "No one's going to believe you forced me to do anything, but you can tell them I didn't have any involve-ment in it."

Usually, I'd quip back, but instead, I just thank him. Then I cross my fingers that I can actually figure out what the hell Grandpa's crystal was doing out here, only a hun-dred feet away from a murder scene.

Chapter 23

By the time we transport back to the school, it's well past midnight. And by the time I make it to my room, my new roommate is fast asleep.

I creep in and climb into bed without changing, falling into the deepest sleep. When I awake, I can't remember dreaming, but I have the heaviest sense of dread that my grandpa did visit me in dreamland and warned me of impending danger again.

I decide I need to use the ring pronto. As per my grandma's instructions, I make sure to slip it on without touching the ruby. Then I pull on a black T-shirt, matching pants, and some boots before heading out to the office to get my class schedule.

As I'm stepping out of my room, I cross paths with my roommate, who's a short girl with curly, brown hair.

"Hey, you must be my roommate." I stick out my hand. "I'm Alana Avery."

"I know who you are." She gives me the nastiest look

207

before shoving by me, stepping into the room and slamming the door in my face.

My lips part in shock. "What the fuck was that about?"

I soon, and very painfully, find out.

I thought, because Jax hasn't treated me differently, it wouldn't bother the Guardians. Boy, oh boy, was I wrong. The entire school officially hates me.

I've been back for only one day, and I've been tripped in the cafeteria, called names, and even my room got trashed. It sucks, but it's not like I don't fight back.

I spent most of my life training to be a fighter, and even though I didn't end up a Keeper, that doesn't mean I don't have a mean right hook. Most of the dudes who tripped me now have pretty, matching black eyes.

Of course, since Vivianne hates the crap out of me, I'm not that surprised when I get called down to the office right before I'm supposed to head to Identifying Otherworldly Creatures class, and I have a feeling I'm about to be in some deep shit.

It takes me almost ten minutes of wandering around in the maze of hallways before I finally find her office. Right as I get there, I cross paths with Jax.

"Where are you going?" Jax asks me as I pass him in the empty hallway. "Don't you have class right now?"

"I got called to Vivianne's office," I say begrudgingly, glaring at her shut office door.

He cocks his head to the side. "That's weird. She usually doesn't call students out of class unless it's something severe."

I twist the ring on my finger. *No, not now. You won't have time to get any answers.* "I may have punched a few guys at lunch today, and she might be a little bit upset by that."

"You punched some guys at lunch?"

"Hey, they tripped me first and were making fun of my grandpa," I argue. "I had to stand up for myself."

He blasts me with a stern look, but a smile sparkles in his eyes. "Vivianne has huge issues with fighting. She's probably going to keep you in the office for the rest of the day and probably make you clean the bathrooms."

"Yippee," I say flatly.

"I'll come check on you later," Jax says, "to make sure you're surviving."

"Don't worry about me. I've had worse punishments." I smile at him. "Wish me luck." Then I turn for the door at the same time he tries to move right to go around me.

We end up colliding, and the ruby grazes his forearm.

"Ah, shit," I curse, jumping back from Jax.

His brows dip as his gaze darts from me to the ring to his arm.

Double ah shit. Does he know what the ring is?

"I have to go," he tells me, still seeming perplexed. "I'll talk to you later."

He wanders down the hallway, scratching his head.

I open my mouth to call him back so I can tell him what happened. I may want to use the ring, but I don't want Jax wandering around and telling everyone his secrets. But Vivianne's office door swings open.

She steps out with an evil grin on her face. "So, I heard you've been causing trouble in my school."

I have no choice except to go inside her office and have a seat.

She sits behind her desk, fixes her bun, and proceeds to scold me for ten minutes straight, looking pleased every second of it. Then she tells me that I'll be spending this week's classes with her.

"Just because you're a Keeper, it doesn't give you the right to inflict violence," she says, giving me a haughty look from across her desk. "You're now a Guardian, and you will start acting like one."

"I was only defending myself." I ball my hands into fists, telling myself to remain calm.

"That's not what I was told." She flips open a folder and reads over a paper inside. "I have a least ten students' written statements that you were the instigator in the fights."

"They're lying, then." I grit my teeth. "They were teasing me that my grandpa's a traitor, and then they tripped me. How is that my fault?"

"Sounds like they were stating facts to me." She closes the folder and pushes back from her desk. "You will complete your assignments in here, along with some of my own assignments." She drops a thick folder down in front of me with a wicked grin on her face. "After the final bell rings, I have some tasks for you to complete outside of the classroom." She stands up, grabs a set of keys from her desk, and crosses the office toward the door. "If you don't finish all the work, I'll add another week to your detention."

She turns her back on me to open the door, and I flip her the middle finger. *She's such a bitch.*

Blowing out a breath, I open the folder filled with papers and grimace. There's no way I'm ever going to be able to finish all of this before the bell rings.

"Oh, good, you made it before I locked up," Vivianne says as she's walking out the door.

I twist around in the chair to see who she's talking to

and am shocked to see Dash, Jax's twin brother, standing in the doorway.

"I told you I'd be here." Dash's casual demeanor matches his tone.

"Yeah, but I never know with you," Vivianne says in a cold voice. "You say one thing and mean another. You hardly follow through with anything."

He crosses his arms, his lips quirking with amusement. "Well, I guess there's a first time for everything."

Vivianne shakes her head. "Whatever. Just make sure she stays in my office, okay?"

"I'll do my best," Dash says with a hint of hilarity in his voice.

"I'm serious, Dash. She may look innocent, but she's been nothing but trouble." Vivianne finds the right key on the keychain. "Her parents are Keepers, too, so don't, under any circumstances, trust her."

"Yes, ma'am." A wicked glint twinkles in his eyes as he looks at me. "If she gives me any trouble, I'll make sure to tie her up and punish her." His eyes darken, and he winks at me.

I roll my tongue, fighting back a laugh.

Vivianne seems oblivious to Dash's teasing tone. "No punishment will be necessary. Just keep her here while I'm out. I shouldn't be longer than an hour." With that, she walks out of the office, shutting the door.

Dash rubs his hands together with an impish grin on his face. "Finally, we're alone."

I giggle. "Finally? You've only known me for, like, a week. And you only talked to me for, like, two minutes."

He rounds the desk and takes a seat in Vivianne's chair, kicking his boots up on the desk. "Yes, but I've been pining over you ever since." He tucks his hands behind his head and singsongs, "The girl with mysterious violet eyes. I can't get her out of my head."

I laugh, shaking my head.

His grin broadens. "It has a nice ring to it, doesn't it?"

"I could totally see it being a song." I pull out the first sheet of paper to get started on the assignments.

He eyes the massive amount of papers in the folder. "Man, she must really not like you."

"Yeah, she hasn't since the first day she met me." I grab a pen from my bag. "Why does she like you so much?"

He elevates a brow. "Who said she does?"

"She has to if she left you in charge of me."

"Only because I'm bound to her."

I press the pen to the paper, but pause. "Bound to her?"

He shrugs, lowering his feet to the floor. "It's a long story."

I wait for him to explain, but instead, he messes around with Vivianne's computer. I hardly know anything about Dash, just that he's not human, has a quirky personality, and smells like sugar. I have no freakin' clue what he is. I could ask, I guess.

As if sensing I'm about to bombard him with questions, he turns on some music loud enough that it's hard to carry-on a conversation.

I decide I better get a move on with the assignments, funnily enough, using a lot of my Keeper knowledge to answer. After I finish the first one, I reach for another.

A second later, Dash grabs one, too, plucks a pen from the cup on the desk, and starts writing answers down.

"You're helping me?" I ask in shock.

He peers up at me innocently. "What do you mean? You did all these by yourself."

I giggle then start jotting down answers as fast as I can. Dash chuckles as his hand moves swiftly across the page. Somehow, it becomes a race.

"I just hope we're getting them all correct," I say after we make it halfway through the stack.

"I don't know if you are, but I guarantee my work is

flawless." He puts the end of the pen between his lips and studies the sheet in front of him with a teasing smile on his face. "The proper way to kill a vampire is to kiss it, right?"

I let out a pig-snort laugh, and his smile expands.

"Well, that was attractive," he says over the music.

I start to quip back, but the office door swings open. I quickly sit up as Dash scrambles to turn off the music, but he stops mid-reach and settles back in the chair with a relaxed look on his face.

"Jax, to what do we owe this pleasure?" Dash says, almost sounding mocking.

When Jax doesn't respond, I set the pen down and turn around in my chair to look at him.

His hair is askew and his eyes wild, as if he's having a mini meltdown.

"I can't get you out of my head," he says to me in a panic.

"Um …" Crappity crap. This has to be because of the ring. I play dumb. "Probably because I'm so annoying, and I irritate the shit out of you."

He shakes his head and kneels down on the floor in front of me. "No, it's not that. I mean … You are annoying, but you're also gorgeous and amazing and really strong. I'm envious of your strength, more than I'll ever admit.

Well, I guess that phrase doesn't really apply anymore since I told you." He pauses, and I cross my fingers that he'll stop talking. Instead, he reaches forward and grazes his knuckles across my cheekbones. "You have such beautiful eyes."

"I ..." I glance at Dash who's watching the scene unfold in wonder.

"Good God, woman, what did you do to my brother?" he says in mock horror.

I rack my brain for a good lie, but I can't think of one. So, I lift my hand up and show him the ring. "Truth Serum."

His brows raise. "You used that on him?"

I nod. "Not intentionally. Well, I was going to use it eventually, but I accidentally bumped into him in the hallway on my way here and now ..." I trail off as Jax rests his head in my lap. "What a disaster! All I wanted was to find out what electi was, not whether or not Jax thinks I'm hot."

"Well, clearly he does," Dash says. "But I could've told you that. The entire week you were gone, he kept yammering about how he hoped you were doing okay."

"Okay, that's kind of sweet," I admit, but then quickly shake my head.

Focus, Alana, focus.

216

Entranced

"So have you," Jax murmurs to his brother. "My obsession with her is more justified, though."

"And how do you figure that?" Dash asks, biting back a grin.

"Because I've talked to her for more than ten seconds," Jax snaps. "But we both know how this will turn out. You'll end up charming her with you laidback, I-don't-give-a-shit-attitude and your stupid cookie smell."

Dash rolls his eyes. "Don't hate the cookie smell just because you smell like a dog."

"I really like this song," I blurt out when Jax lets out a growl and starts to raise his head from my lap. "It's got a cool ring to it."

"It's okay." Jax lifts his head to look at me. "I could stare at you all day."

Dash laughs, and I fight back an eye roll at the cheesiness. *Stop laughing at him! This is all your fault!*

I absentmindedly comb my fingers through his hair and when he lets out a moan, I jerk back. "Jax, what's electi mean?" I try to get him focused on something else.

He sighs. "I told you to stop asking about that... I need to protect you. But now I feel like I have to tell you, and it's going to be so bad." He sucks in an inhale. "Electi are the people running the paranormal experimental facilities. No one's supposed to know about them, and they kill anyone who finds out about them. I've just recently learned about them while I was investigating a murder, but I think they're linked to several murders. I don't know why they're killing so many creatures, though... So far, they don't know that I know, but I'm not sure how long I'll stay off their radar. And if they get ahold of me, they'll probably use me for one of their experiments since I'm a werewolf … And now you know about them, too." He shudders. "This is so bad."

This is definitely so bad. More than bad.

Why was my grandpa talking to these people right before he died? Why did he warn me about them?

And if he really is dead, are they the ones who killed him?

Chapter 24

It takes about an hour for the Truth Serum to wear off. In that time, Jax talks nonstop and even tries to kiss me a couple of times. It finally gets so bad Dash ties him to a chair and cranks up the music, trying to keep some of his secrets a secret, which I'm grateful for. The last thing I ever wanted to know is that Jax was turned on by my snippy attitude when we first met each other back at the Black Dungeon. He was so turned on he had to take a cold shower after he left.

"You're kind of a troublemaker," Dash says as Jax finally grows quiet, slowly coming out of his trance.

"I just needed to know what Electi is, and he knew but refused to tell me." I feel like such an asshole. "I didn't mean for it to get this out of hand."

He waves me off. "I didn't mean it in a bad way. In fact, I respect it." He winks at me as he gets up to untie a very dazed out Jax. "I would've done the same thing if I were in your situation."

"I'm not sure whether to take that as a compliment or not," I say, writing the last answer on the final sheet.

He grins. "Definitely a compliment. Everyone wants to be like me. I promise."

"What on earth is going on in here?" Vivianne storms into her office, shouting over the music. "Dash, turn that music down."

He does what she says and hurries to move out of her chair. "Sorry, but I couldn't help myself. You have such lovely taste in music." He tries to charm her.

Vivianne hovers between irritated and smitten and glances at Jax, who is half out of it. "Why is he in here? I said not to let anyone in."

"My brother had to pass along a message from my parents since I left my phone in my room," Dash lies easily. "He's been sick, though, and so I told him to rest here before heading out to his next assignment."

Vivianne looks unconvinced, but she still lets him off the hook, telling him to go and take Jax with him.

After they leave, she checks over my assignments then sends me to clean the bathrooms under the supervision of the janitor.

"And, Alana," she calls out before I leave. "Tomorrow morning, you are to come straight to my office for another day of detention. This time, you will not be under the supervision of Dash, nor will he be helping you with your assignments." Her tone carries a warning, letting me know tomorrow is going to be much worse than today.

I nod then head to the cleaning closet with the janitor to get supplies. I spend hours cleaning. There are a total of twelve bathrooms in the school—yes, twelve—and I have to scrub down all of them. Not only is it gross, but by the time I get back to my room, it's nearing midnight.

Before I go in, I try to call my grandma to tell her what I found out, but then I pause. Jax said these people kill anyone who finds out about them. If I tell my grandma, then I put her at risk.

I hang up without calling. I can't tell her and put her in danger like that, not until I find out more.

Putting my phone into my pocket, I slip into my room, surprised to find my roommate's bed empty. It's way past curfew. I wonder where she could be.

I'm too tired to stress out over it, though, so I change into my pajamas and climb into bed.

What a first day. Seriously. Hopefully, it won't always be like this, but I have a feeling that, as long as Vivianne is in charge, I'll be under constant scrutiny.

I stare at the moon as I fall asleep, thinking about Jax

and wondering how mad at me he's going to be tomorrow morning. Probably really, really pissed off. With any luck, he won't remember everything he told me.

My eyelashes flutter shut as I yawn and start to drift asleep.

"Don't close your eyes yet, Alana," my grandpa whispers. "They're coming for you. They're coming for all of you. They want every creature they can find."

"What for?" I ask. "Grandpa, please tell me why you were talking to the Electi."

"Because they wanted me on their side ... They wanted me to help them build an army ..."

"You should've left it alone," someone whispers.

My eyelids fly open as I bolt upright in my bed. My fingers fumble to turn the lamp on, and then my gaze frantically skims the room. Nothing seems out of the ordinary except that the door is cracked open.

I throw my blanket off, grab the nearest object that will work as a weapon—my roommate's baseball bat—then pad over to the door. With the bat raised, I open the door, stick my head out into the hallway, and my heart slams against my chest.

Painted across the tile floor is a serpent shaped in a backward three.

I glance up and down the hallway, but there's no sign of anyone anywhere.

Why is it here?

"Because they know you know, my grandpa whispers inside my head. *Be careful, Alana. Be very, very careful. If they're watching you, then they don't want to kill you. They want you."*

I think about what Jax told me, how the Electi wouldn't kill him because he was a werewolf, but they would experiment on him.

"But what do they want with me?" I ask.

Instead of hearing his answers, a door bangs shut from somewhere. I scramble back into my room, and lock the door, my heart thrashing in my chest.

I need to figure out what the hell is going on. I just hope I can before the Electi get me.

About the Author

Jessica Sorensen is a *New York Times* and *USA Today* bestselling author who lives in the snowy mountains of Wyoming. When she's not writing, she spends her time reading and hanging out with her family.

Other books by Jessica Sorensen:

<u>Guardian Academy Series:</u>

Entranced (Guardian Academy, Book One)

Entangled (Guardian Academy, Book 2) (Coming Soon)

<u>Rebels & Misfits Series:</u>

Confessions of a Kleptomaniac

<u>Honeyton Series:</u>

The Illusion of Annabella

Sunnyvale Series:

The Year I Became Isabella Anders

The Year of Falling In Love (Coming Soon)

The Coincidence Series:

The Coincidence of Callie and Kayden

The Redemption of Callie and Kayden

The Destiny of Violet and Luke

The Probability of Violet and Luke

The Certainty of Violet and Luke

The Resolution of Callie and Kayden

Seth & Greyson

The Secret Series:

The Prelude of Ella and Micha

The Secret of Ella and Micha

The Forever of Ella and Micha

The Temptation of Lila and Ethan

Entranced

The Ever After of Ella and Micha

Lila and Ethan: Forever and Always

Ella and Micha: Infinitely and Always

The Shattered Promises Series:

Shattered Promises

Fractured Souls

Unbroken

Broken Visions

Scattered Ashes

Breaking Nova Series:

Breaking Nova

Saving Quinton

Delilah: The Making of Red

Nova and Quinton: No Regrets

Tristan: Finding Hope

Wreck Me

Ruin Me

The Fallen Star Series (YA):

The Fallen Star

The Underworld

The Vision

The Promise

The Fallen Souls Series (spin off from The Fallen Star):

The Lost Soul

The Evanescence

The Darkness Falls Series:

Darkness Falls

Darkness Breaks

Darkness Fades

The Death Collectors Series (NA and YA):

Entranced

Ember X and Ember

Cinder X and Cinder

Spark X and Cinder

The Sins Series:

Seduction & Temptation

Sins & Secrets

Unbeautiful Series:

Unbeautiful

Untamed